MW01251865

JINX
MOTHER CHAPTER
FLORA BURGOS

Cover Designed by Tracie Douglas at Dark Water Covers

Formatting by LJ Stock at LJ Designs

Edited by Julia Goda at Diamond In The Rough Editing

Because laughter opens and frees from rigid preconception, humans had to have tricksters within the most sacred ceremonies for fear that they forget the sacred comes through upset, reversal, surprise.

Byrd Gibbens

DEDICATION

Shelene,

Thank you for being my sister from another mister. Thank you for always having my back and being there, rather it's letting me rant about something or breaking the monotony of another long and busy day with random facts or feedback. Thank you for being you. When God was handing out ride or dies, he knew I needed you.

I love you,
Flora

ACKNOWLEDGMENTS

Abby, my beautiful and supremely talented niece, thank you for taking my brief and rambling description of what I envisioned as the club logo, and not only bringing it to life but making it better than I could have ever imagined. You are amazing, and I cannot wait to see where your art takes you!

Alex(andrea) the Awesome. I love the shit out of you. You've been with me through every single book and you are an integral part of my team. You give it to me truthfully and always have my books and their best interests at heart. You are one of the strongest and most beautiful souls that I know and I am never letting you go. You see and understand a part of my soul that very few do and you have no idea how special that is to me. I am so proud of you. You know why. You are a badass, you are amazing and I never want to do this without you. Ever.

Tracie, Tracie, Tracie, what would I do without you? You make me all these crazy amazing covers and are drawing me in with these pre-mades and making story after story flow.

Julia!! The acknowledgements are always the last thing I write before sending you my manuscript, so this is how you know that I'm done tweaking and changing things. I know, I know. Enough is enough. I'm lol'ing right now. You have the patience of a saint!

Cindy, without you I wouldn't be me and without Tree I wouldn't have known the first thing about bikers. You gave me a chance and you are a big part of the reason that I have this amazing life I lead. Thank you for being an inspiration, a badass and one of the strongest women I know. You never, not once, did anything in halves for your half-sister. I will never find the words to tell you the difference you made for me. I'm here because of you. I adore you.

Rolando, my gorgeous, supportive, rock of a husband, thank you for being in my corner, encouraging me to chase my dreams, and being the best father and husband your son and I could ever ask for. Were it not for you, this would be nothing but a dream. This has been a crazy year for us Babycakes. You've taken this roller coaster ride with me and kept me sane and healthy through it all. You believe in me, support me, and love me through the good days and the bad. When I laid my head down at night before you, my prayer was for someone who loved me unconditionally. When I lay my head down at night now? I thank Him for giving me you and all the blessings you brought into my life.

Hopefully, you never read Mama's books, but T, thank you. Thank you for being your amazing, happy and caring self. For being like your dad and reminding me to drink water and eat when I've been at my computer for hours, and for being like me and still seeing all the good in the world, even for all the tragedy. You are my greatest blessing. You and your daddy are my everything.

Shout out to my tribe for having my back always, for getting me through my first two book signings, for letting me be me, and for doing everything that you do to make my books possible.

Thank you to every reader who picks up this book and gives it a chance. I will never reach a point when I am not grateful for every bit of my ability to weave a story, share it with you all, and have someone somewhere pick it up and fall in love. Having this in my life is more fulfilling and more wonderful that I could have ever hoped for.

PROLOGUE

Roxanne

As if Mother Nature had taken it upon herself to prove a point, the torrential rain was lashing sideways, and the wind was howling with an intensity that whistled eerily against the dilapidated, rundown single-wide. I was right back where I'd promised I would never go again and I kind of hated myself for caving.

I didn't know it yet, but before the end of the day, my life would be veering sharply off course.

I was late for my morning class at Delaney Community College because I'd had to rush home to walk my dog before I could leave him locked inside all day. Typically, this was the first thing on my to-do list in the morning, but I hadn't spent the night before at my place, because I was an idiot, and he had been stuck inside all night. I felt like a horrible dog mom. Luckily for me, my boy was a patient one, and waiting on me was way better than the reality he'd known not so long ago. It was a huge inconvenience to be so far away and a pretty crappy start to my day, but it was nowhere near as bad as it could've been.

The night before, I'd just finished up with one of my

yoga videos and was attempting to find the Zen feeling you're supposed to get from doing yoga when my phone rang. Hearing the ringtone, I rolled my eyes.

Of course.

Norman and I had a routine. I would get fed up and have enough of his shit and tell him we were over; then he would take a couple of days to screw anything that walked and then call me repentant and begging for me to take him back.

Last time I'd vowed that it was the *last* time, but then I'd made the stupid, stupid, *stupid* mistake of answering my phone when he called, and there he was: same song and dance, and same reaction from me.

This time, he was swearing that he couldn't live without me, this was our longest separation in the three years we'd been together—so far, I'd made it six weeks—and he threatened to kill himself. I would like to say that I threw my hands in the air and let it go, but really, at the end of the day, who wants someone else's death on their conscience?

So, of course, I caved and agreed to come over already knowing it was a mistake.

When I walked through the door, he reached out and roughly pushed me against the wall. He was in a hurry to get me inside before I could change my mind, and fear and desperation were all over his face. The disgusting, nauseating smell of marijuana mixed with what could only be spoiled food left in the trash for days made bile rear up in my throat.

If I wasn't there to keep his life ordered for him, his house clean, his laundry done, setting the bills out and reminding him about them repeatedly so they would get paid, then none of it was taken care of. He looked like he hadn't showered in days, and I was sure he was coming down from a bender on his latest drug of choice, whatever that was. He had hit all the basics with cocaine and meth and then his favorite: heroin.

Norm was a formidable man, but I had to admit that the thing that had kept me coming back was that he wasn't physically abusive to a point I couldn't take, and he *needed* me. I was an orphan, an unwanted drain on the world whose life had started on the dirty, rotten floor of a derelict, abandoned crack house; according to the police report anyway, and had only been more of the same after. I bounced around the system from foster home to foster home.

Living with people who only wanted free labor and a government paycheck, or worse. Norman, though? He'd made me feel needed and loved. The desperate obsession he had with me had provided comfort in the beginning, a codependency, really, which had eventually started to wear on me until we ended up here.

Tears were streaming from his eyes—him, this man who scared other people, a blight on society who peddled drugs to the high school and college kids in our town, some of them who were or had been my classmates. Here he was on his knees in front of where I sat on the couch, and through the shuddering tears, he sobbed, "Roxy, can't live without you. Ain't no point. If I can't be with you, then you might as well take a gun and shoot me dead." I rolled my eyes at this. He was so dramatic when he was riding a high. He couldn't handle his drugs any better than he could his alcohol, and he was worse than the girl who drank too much, threw up on the dance floor, and then spent the night crying.

Instead of saying anything sarcastic, no matter how intense

the urge was, I murmured softly, "Hey, it's okay." What else could I say? I couldn't commit to anything. I wanted to be anywhere other than where I sat but not knowing what chemical he had dabbled with this time, that wasn't a chance I was willing to take. He could react with more tears or snap into anger and rage for hours.

Luckily, he took this as some sort of confirmation and looked at me, whispering, "Yeah?"

Again, there wasn't a single thing I could say to convey my true feelings, so I faked a smile and fought the roiling pitch of nausea in my gut as I whispered, "Yeah."

My lie seemed to open the floodgates for him as even more tears flooded his face and he walked on his knees to me before climbing on the couch and giving me no choice but to lean back and let him curl into me. All I had to offer to this shell of a man were placating sounds with no real commitment behind them; I couldn't and wouldn't make any more promises to him. I'd known for a while that I needed a change, and this was further cementing it for me. Not only did I no longer enjoy his desperation for me, but I was also beginning to hate him for being so weak and stupid. Over and over again, he chose this lifestyle; the drugs, and the highs and the lows that came with them. When combined with the addictive thrill of danger, I knew that he was never going to change. And I'd already had my fill of it all long before meeting him, so there was no way I could spend the rest of my life caught in this pattern.

I knew this, yet still, we ended up with me sitting on the couch, his head resting on my breast while he cried like a newborn, gasping for breath on the inhale and my shirt gripped tightly in his fist.

I needed to getaway.

This whole sick cycle had to end for my sanity, no matter how many times he called and begged or what threats he made.

I. Was. Done.

Done.

When I got the chance this time, I was out of here, and I would never step foot through his door again.

I tried to outwait him. I watched as the second-hand circled time and again on the clock hanging on his wall. I doubted it was even set to the correct time, but still, those hands taunted me as time ticked by as slowly as it ever had in my life and I silently cursed myself for not changing my damn number before I nodded off.

I was yanked into awareness when I felt him drop a blanket over me and heard him silence a ringing phone; it wasn't his standard ringtone, so I had to figure it was the one he had called me from that was unknown — drug line. I continued to feign sleep until I heard him start up the shower— he must have finally come down from his high—and I waited a few more moments just to be sure before I lurched up and ran out the door to my car. I needed a change, and it was beginning right now. I needed to get the hell out of Dodge and start over somewhere different with no ties; where no one saw me as the girl who was hooked up to the local drug dealer and loser.

I slammed into my car and fumbled the keys before getting the car started and threw it in gear when my phone started ringing, telling me that I hadn't made as clean of a getaway as I'd hoped.

He would expect me to answer like I always had, but I knew better. I was working on an escape plan, and there was no way he was going to have the chance to draw me back in again. I realized just how ironic this was a few short hours later, when Norman's mother, who was surprisingly normal, given how disturbed her son was, came beating on my door.

Her, I would open the door for, and did, even though I quickly came to regret it. As the older woman shoved into the door and pushed past me, she was already mid-rant. "Damn conspiracy is what it is. My boy has been gettin' clean. He's been goin' to those meetin's every week, just like his probation officer told him to. We gotta get him out of there."

"Wha-what on earth are you talking about?"

"Girl, I'm telling you! The poh-lice showed up and took Norm to jail for possession and intent to distribute. I can't afford to bail him out, so you gotta get your checkbook so we can get down there and get him out of there."

I had never been so happy that I was living in a paycheck-to-paycheck world before in my life. "Miss Linda, I can't do that. I don't have any money."

"Well, shit." She looked up at the ceiling and huffed out a breath. "I don't know what to tell him then. I ain't got it."

I started to edge her toward the door. I didn't think that she knew about the dog, but it wouldn't be good for my canine roommate to come out now. I needed her out of here as soon as humanly possible.

She was almost there, just a few feet from the door, when she threw her arms around me, a surprising moment of emotion from her on my behalf, "What are you going to do, Roxanne? If he goes down, you won't have anyone!" The last part she wailed in my ear.

Once more, I found myself comforting someone else,

nonsensical words and all, before finally, I was able to coerce her out the door. Shutting it behind her, I sighed in relief.

When all was said and done, Norman was going to spend eighteen months in prison, and I was planning to use this to my benefit and get the hell out of there while I could. I had loose ends that I was going to tie up as fast as humanly possible, and graduation was only weeks away.

By the time I was supposed to be crossing the stage, Norman would be serving his sentence, and my dog and I would be long gone.

I got a Post Office box to forward my mail to, talked to my professors, and managed to fast track my work and finish my finals before the due dates. Then I sold and gave away everything that I didn't absolutely have to have. There was nothing left for me here and no reason to carry my second and third-hand belongings to wherever I ended up. It would be way smarter to pack light and only take the essentials.

By the time Norman was free and able to begin his life once more, I had found myself in a whole other state on the opposite side of the country, in a completely different kind of trouble, with far deadlier repercussions.

I had a knack for that.

Jumping from the frying pan to the fire.

CHAPTER ONE

Roxanne

Sixteen months later

I'd only just crossed over the bridge onto Galveston Island when my car gave a couple of coughs, and the engine died.

Luckily, I was able to pull to the side of the road from momentum alone, and as I pulled on the e-brake on the shoulder of a mostly abandoned road at an ungodly hour of the morning, I knew that my time as a drifter had come at an end. I couldn't justify going any further when I had reached the opposite end of the country. I just had no clue what I was going to do now.

I grabbed my cell from my bag and checked, but I had no battery; it was completely dead, as usual. Not that I knew anybody I could call anyway. In frustration, I bumped my head against the steering wheel and muttered a mantra of "Fuck, fuck, fuck" every time my forehead connected with the steering wheel under my hands. Zeus, my Pitbull, whined and licked my cheek, distracting me from braining myself.

Before getting out of the car, I popped the release lever under my steering wheel, then quickly shut the door, leaving my window cracked just a hair so Zeus could get fresh air.

It was dark out, so I had to fumble to find the latch to release the hood. Lifting it to see the motor didn't do me any good though because I had no clue what I was looking at or for.

I knew that somewhere in there was a thing that held the water—and I even knew how to add more, though only if the engine was off and wasn't hot. And there was something in there that contained oil and some other fluids that they refilled when I could afford to and took my car in for a tire rotation and whatnot, but that was all I could say with any certainty. With no other options save getting my dog out and walking, I left the hood propped open and got back into the car.

That was the universal signal for help, right?

Besides, I had a nine-millimeter in the center console, and thinking about it, I took it out and dropped the mag into my lap before aiming the weapon at the ground between my feet and pulling the slide back and forth quickly a few times to eject a bullet on the off chance I left it loaded last time. I grinned like a moron even as I hoped that I looked as badass as I felt every time I did it.

It always gave me a thrill; but, I knew it was essential to check every single time to be absolutely sure. It'd be a tragedy to think it was loaded and try to defend myself, only to find that my gun wouldn't fire.

Satisfied that the chamber was empty, I shoved the mag loaded with bullets back into the gun and pulled the slide once more to ensure it was good to go if my safety was in question. I grinned. Yep, I totally felt like a badass.

I pushed the button to turn on the safety, thereby locking

the trigger the I hit the lock button on my door to double-check that the doors were locked.

I turned the key to lower the windows just slightly more than they already were, reclined my seat, and tried to close my eyes. There was nothing for it. I'd have to wait until someone decided to drive by and stop to help or call for a tow, which I would have to figure out how to afford. This certainly wouldn't be the first or last time we had spent all night, or what was left of it, in my car, so my boy did a couple of circles on the backseat and then lay down snuggled into his blanket.

It felt like decades, sitting uneasily on the side of the highway waiting for someone to stop, but really it was probably only an hour or two, as the sun still hadn't risen through the clouds all the way when I heard the roar of motorcycle pipes roll up behind me. Traffic had picked up a little, but not a soul had stopped, so my heart rate spiked up as my internal danger alarm went off. My four-ways were still flashing, theoretically drawing attention to my car, so all I could do was pray the biker that stopped wouldn't end up killing me for the effort because someone could witness it.

I unlocked the door and moved to step out of my car, shoving the pistol into the back of my waistband on my jeans. I had just closed the door and wiped my hands on my thighs when Zeus jumped to attention and let out warning barks as the motorcycle slowed to a stop right behind my car. I shaded my eyes from the bright light beaming from the front of his bike as the driver cut the engine and removed his helmet. It was hard to make out my would-be rescuer (or murderer) in the quiet almost-dark stillness of the very early morning after the light on his bike died out, and I jumped when he spoke.

"Engine trouble?"

His voice was raspy and sexy in a way that scrambled my thoughts and caused my belly to flutter and thighs to quiver while I felt the chill of fear race down my spine in a confusing set of opposing reactions. So when I spoke, of course, I sounded ridiculous. "Um, well, I think so? My car just kinda coughed and died, and I had just enough momentum to pull it to the shoulder. I, ah, popped the hood, but I have to be honest with you. I know how to put gas in my car and run it through the car wash, but that's about it. I pay someone else to see to the rest of it."

The biker took a pack of cigarettes out of his pocket, and I watched as he shook one out while I was speaking. I thought I saw his lips curl up as he lit his square silver lighter and held the flame to the tip. He closed the lighter and put it away and then brought his hand up to take the lit cigarette from his mouth and spoke on his exhale.

"Let's see what you got going on here."

As he approached my car, the giant teddy bear in my backseat let out a warning bark accompanied by a low growl. The biker paused for a second in his stride to the front of my car while I hushed Zeus.

"It's ok, baby. He's helping Mommy with her car. Just relax, big guy; we'll be out of here shortly."

The big guy (human this time) barked a laugh in surprise, and I quickly looked his way.

"Big-ass dog, babe. You from around here?"

It took me a second to catch up to what he was asking with his rapid-fire subject change. "Nope, not even close. We're taking a hiatus of sorts from life and made our way here in a roundabout way from Seattle."

"Hmm." He said weirdly before throwing me off-kilter again, "You sticking around today and got a place to stay tonight?"

"Not really, I didn't know where we would end up tonight, so I just planned to catch a few in my car."

"Alright, let's take a look. Hop in and try to turn her over."

I did as I was told, but when I opened the door, I had to push my overenthusiastic dog back into the backseat, so I was distracted and unprepared. As I was bent over, the tail of my shirt raised, exposing the small of my back, I felt cool air hit my skin as the man yanked my pistol from my waistband.

My heart stuttered in panic as I felt him pull it free, but as I jerked around as quickly as I could in my panicked state, I saw that he was only holding the weapon out with his hand on the barrel for me to take the butt.

"Better mind that gun before you shoot yourself." If I wasn't mistaken, this stranger was chastising me. *What the hell.*

I snatched the gun from his hand and rested my pointer finger along the barrel while holding it at my side. My chest was rapidly rising and falling with adrenalin, and I was dizzy with the realization that he hadn't turned it on me. I hopped in my car, slightly miffed and a whole lot relieved, as he swaggered back to the front. I sat the gun down in my passenger seat and put my foot on the break. I figured that by giving me my gun back, he was assuring me that I was ok, at least for the time being.

"Turn 'er over," he said to me.

I turned the key, and the car made a gurgling noise while it turned over and over, not catching.

"Whoa," he shouted back to me over the noise, "hang on a sec!"

I let go of the key, took my foot off the brake, and waited for his next command.

He fiddled with some stuff under the hood and then shouted back to me, "Ok, try it again!"

When I turned the key this time, the engine made a weird sound and then finally, *finally* caught.

"Woo-hoo!" I shouted and did a little boogie in my seat, to which my boy barked in excitement and wagged his tail, panting happily.

I hopped out of the car and slammed the door, and in my excitement, I acted like a total moron and ran to, then threw my arms around the big, muscled, hairy bulk of a man who only a few moments ago had me quaking in my Converse. The man in question stiffened in my embrace in surprise and then gave me an awkward back pat before I released him, embarrassment finally sinking in.

"Sorry! I just knew that Sally would never purr again! I owe you big, *huge*, whatever you want! My firstborn? Yours. My eternal gratitude? You got it. Oh! I can give you the change in my console! I'm not carrying cash, so I can't give you that, but anything else is yours!" I turned to my car to gather the change I had to offer him for his kindness, but he stopped me with his words.

"Sweetness, I don't want anything. Anyone who drove past you would've stopped. You get into town and get somewhere safe until the sun comes up, and that'll work as repayment. You don't need to be sleeping in your car, especially not in this town, regardless of the loaded piece and big-ass scary-looking dog."

"You got it. I'll stop at the first motel I come across and book it for tonight!" I motioned as if I were checking it off an invisible to-do list.

The biker stepped back and took me in in the light of the early morning sun. I'm sure I looked a sight, what with my hair pulled up in a sloppy bun, wearing an oversized Henley, my flannel pajama shorts paired with my hot-pink Converse, and driving a convertible Mustang with a loud, drooling Pitbull in the small, cramped backseat. He shook his head with a grin and stuck out his hand, offering to shake mine while saying, "I'm headed into town myself and can follow you to one of the motels to be certain you don't break down again. You're going to need someone to take a look at your car before you attempt to go any further because I'm thinking you need a new fuel pump. Name's Jinx, by the way." He stuck out his hand.

I held my palm out and took it while saying, "Thank you for everything, Jinx. I'm Roxanne."

After he released my hand, I paused awkwardly, staring at him, before my brain kicked in, and I grinned at him and waved awkwardly before hopping back in the car and starting off once again in the direction I had been aiming.

I turned my blinker on and pulled back onto the highway when I heard the loud bike roar to life and watched in the rearview mirror as the seriously sexy man who had magically, even if only temporarily, fixed my car, followed me to the city limits. Looking back as I pulled into the parking lot of the first decent-looking motel I came across, I saw the man flick his arm out in a low wave before he roared past.

Part of me, a big part, wanted to follow him to wherever he went and throw myself at him; but, sanity prevailed, and I instead put my car into park.

He had no idea that I waited only moments after he pulled away before I pulled out of the parking lot and headed the same direction he took, hoping to find somewhere along the beach where I could pull off and park to catch some sleep before the city came fully awake and I had to move once more.

CHAPTER TWO

Roxanne

I should have known that if I ever saw the sexy biker again, it would be under equally embarrassing circumstances.

It was just my luck.

So when I rolled into Double M Bikes, Auto & Diesel, a garage recommended to me by an older man with long, scruffy gray hair who was sitting on the seawall smoking what I was reasonably sure was a joint, while I was taking my boy for a walk this morning, I was wearing the only clean clothes I owned. An embarrassing outfit which just so happened to be cutoff shorts, my hot-pink Converse, and a tank that read "Sun's out, Guns out" and had a tear on the side where I had the fabric twisted into a knot (also known as my laundry-day outfit). My hair was in a ratty bun that hadn't seen a brush in a good twenty-four hours, and I had not a trace of makeup with my huge Dollar Store sunglasses covering my eyes. The scary-looking guy at the front desk called out when I walked through the door, "Yo, darlin', what can I do for you?"

I had no idea that my life was about to be set onto another path.

If the day Norm got arrested had set me on my course,

then today was the precipice where it all changed once more. Although truthfully, I suppose you could say that had actually happened last night and at an ungodly hour this morning.

I mean, honestly, I was just minding my business when my life was thrown off its axis.

I made my way to him feeling awkward and insecure when I spoke up, "I had some car trouble last night. I think the guy said it was my fuel gauge or gas pump thingy or something? Anyways, I need to get someone to take a look at it and see if you all can figure out what the problem is and how much it's going to cost. I, ah, don't have much cash on me, so I need to see where I am cost-wise before I commit. Is that, like, a thing? Can you triage my car for me?"

He started to speak as the door that led from the car bays into the lobby opened, and I heard a vaguely familiar voice call out, "We got a call out to tow one in, and I ain't got the time. Gonna need you to take care of that, yeah?" The guy who had opened his mouth to speak turned toward the door and instead answered the male speaker.

"Sure thing. We got someone here who needs a triage"—I swear he snickered here—"on her ride. Says it's the fuel gauge or gas pump *thingy*; she's not sure which."

As he spoke, the face behind that familiar voice came around the corner, and I got my first eyeful of Jinx in full on daylight. Man, oh man, was he gorgeous, which for some reason caused me to become a stupefied drooling mess. Those flutters from the night before felt like they had taken a massive dose of performance-enhancing drugs and were now massive gargoyles.

"Didn't expect to see you but glad to see you brought your

car in like I told you."

I'm pretty sure I was supposed to respond here, but hello, I was in a sexy trance or something.

It was like one of those commercials where the chick swings her hair in slow motion. Yeah, it felt exactly like that, apart from the fact Jinx was no longer moving, and I was staring still in awe of him and not saying a word or even so much as daring to breathe.

"Yo," he called.

"Sweetness?" he tried again.

Nada.

Finally, it was my name said on a laugh that snapped me out of it. "Roxanne?"

Of course, my reaction wasn't lost on anyone, so the other guy was snickering again, and I had to do a quick chin swipe to make sure I wasn't drooling.

Which only served to embarrass me further.

My mortification knew no ends, but finally, I just had to set my shoulders and sally forth.

"Hey, Jinx. Umm, you said something about my gas thingymajig, so I wanted to find somewhere to get it checked, and there was an old man smoking weed on the seawall who said you guys were the best, so here I am, to see what's going on and how much I was going to have to save up to fix it." Unless it was free, it was going to hurt, but I didn't want him to know that.

Jinx froze for a second, and then I saw his bearded face break into a grin.

"Yeah, Sweetness, your gas thingymajig." He winked.

I could tell he was laughing at me, which made me even

more embarrassed, so I copped a bit of an attitude when I responded with, "Yeah, that. So, can you do that, or should I go somewhere else?"

"You got that monster in your ride? Cuz if so, I gotta tell you, none of the boys are gonna feel real safe messing around with it."

"My baby is not a monster! He is a sweetheart and loves his mommy." And he was a big scary biker. I mentally rolled my eyes.

"Yeah, sweetheart Pit-fuckin-bull. I'm sure he'll lick you to death, yeah? Those barks and growls this morning coming from your backseat an offer of friendship?"

Ok, now the asshole was pissing me off. Nothing got to me quicker than someone judging my guy because of their own bias. Goodbye, gargoyle flutters; hello, snarling mama bear. "I will have you know that I rescued him from my ex, who just so happened to be a drug dealer. He took him home, locked him in a tiny pen, and bragged about a dogfighting ring. I didn't honestly believe him, but when I saw the dog bloody and hurt really, really badly a few days later, I stole him, took him to the vet to get help and swore to the stupid ex that I had no idea what happened. And just FYI," I was full-blown ranting and couldn't stop myself, "it was not easy to keep him from coming to my house as I was hiding his "prizefighter" there. Also, those vet bills were stupid expensive." Dammit! Word vomit.

He gaped at me for a second, jaw hanging, before he threw his head back and roared in laughter, "Sweetness, there is a lot there that needs some explainin', but for now, yes or no, you got that monster in your car, or is it terrorizing the girls down at the motel?"

"Yes, of course, I have him in my car. Would you leave your children alone in a strange motel room?" I snapped at him.

He studied me for a second before lobbing back at me, "I don't have kids, four-legged or otherwise; but just saying, I wouldn't leave 'em in the car if I did. Now, what did you plan to do with the unholy terror while we look at your car?"

"I'm going to take him for a walk. Get acquainted with the area and maybe see if I can find somewhere that sells ice cream. Then I need to get a job making some cake to get my car fixed. I don't like to make plans, so besides that, I've got nothing."

If I knew him better, or say at all, I would think the look that crossed his face was scheming, but I didn't so I couldn't say for sure, "Right. Well, Sweetness, get the monster out and toss me your keys, and I'll take another look. Gotta say, though, that I'm pretty certain I know what's wrong, and a fuel pump even at cost is gonna cost a fuckin' whack. You keep hobbling along, and it's gonna give out on you in a permanent sort of way, and you and your monster will be hoofing it."

I forgot all about his face entirely when I looked up at the ceiling and prayed for some patience before giving up, and instead shouted at him. "My baby is *not a monster*, and my name is *Roxanne*, not Sweetness!" I almost stomped my foot before I thought better of it. Of course, the big freaking jerk laughed again.

Jinx followed me out to the car, so I could get Zeus out and hand him the keys. Since he was well trained, all I had to do was open the door, push the driver's seat forward, and say, "Come." He calmly exited the car and stood at my feet, tail wagging, leash dragging on the ground. I reached down and picked it up, slipping my right hand through the loop, and said, "Sit." His large doggie bottom dropped to the pavement, and his tail wagged lazily as he waited to see what I would say next.

Jinx let out a low whistle, and when I met his eyes, he was giving me an appraising look. "Little thing like you, and that dog looks like he's seen death up close and personal, not to mention he has got to outweigh you by a good twenty-five pounds, yet there he is, happy as a clam."

"I tried to tell you he isn't a monster. He's a very well-trained and intelligent guy and will do whatever I ask of him."

"So, how on earth did you rescue it from a druggie ex with a dogfighting ring and then get 'im trained so well?"

I debated blowing off his question, but that word vomit erupted again, so I found myself rambling against my will, "About a year and a half ago, druggie ex, AKA Norman, was locked up because his little habit got him busted, so I finished my classes, graduated, packed my shit, and hit the road. I found out in the first five hundred miles that keeping a high-energy animal cooped up with no manners was just not going to cut it, so we had a two-month stay over in Missoula, where I worked him with a K-9 trainer until he got to the point that I could work with him solo, then we took off again. The next several months, I worked with him every time we stopped; and even if you don't know where you're going, you still have to stop for bathroom breaks, gas, food, and the occasional temporary gig for cash. And now we've been on the road a while and are perfectly content."

"So, you set out with your degree, big-ass dog, and essentially the clothes on your back? How does that work? No family looking for you?"

I let out a bitter laugh. I wasn't used to discussing my family or lack thereof. It was intrusive and quite frankly none of his business. I had told him too much already, but I answered, regardless. "I came up in the system. No family to speak of, stumbled into a relationship with the local drug dealer at my last high school and couldn't get out of it. Waited till he was locked up and got the hell outta there."

Jinx's jaw had hardened while I was talking. I had no clue why. I waited, suddenly feeling nervous and unsure what his body language was saying, but it freaked me way the hell out.

After several tense moments, he spoke, and it wasn't anything I could have expected. "Degree?"

"I'm sorry?"

"You got your degree?"

"Umm, yeah?"

"In?"

"In what?" Why on earth was he so confusing?

"Yes, in what?"

"Wait. What?" I was lost.

"Degree, Sweetness. What's it in?"

Again, why was he so confusing? "Liberal Arts."

"What's the fuckin point of that?"

"Well, free college and no real idea about what I wanted to be when I grew up? I didn't know I was going to be quizzed on it!" Jesus, he was getting on my last nerve with this.

His lips twitched before once again going severe, and he asked, "How long've you paid up at the motel?"

Now, that was something I was not responding to. I didn't know much about this biker, but that was more personal than I was willing to get and not any of his business for that matter. Taking a moment to think about it, I had no clue why I had revealed everything I had to him in the short time I had known him. Now I was questioning the decision to tell him that I was virtually alone in the world except for a drooling overweight dog.

"Why are you asking me these questions? If I die, there are still people who will be looking for me." *Not that I want them to find me*, I added mentally.

His angry expression had disappeared, and suddenly he looked on the verge of laughter again, "Sweetness. How long are you paid up at the motel?"

I answered without considering it any further, "I'm covered for a couple of weeks if I need it." Lies.

"Right. Well, seeing as the monster is behaving, you need a way to make some money, and I got a way for you to do that, you fill out one of those applications we got behind the counter and start greeting people when they walk in and scheduling them, and Friday you can have your first paycheck. Also, I got a house that has a spare room you can stay in and that *monster*"—this time he put extra emphasis on that word—"can stay with you as long as he don't tear shit up and is housebroken."

I stared at this man who for all his good looks had to be a stark raving lunatic, because who in the heck would offer a random woman not only a job but a room to stay in, for what I was assuming would be free? And could I look any rattier than I did today?

Yeah, possibly this morning when he saw me stranded on the side of the road. For all this man knew, I may not even own any decent clothes!

"Sweetness, you with me?"

"Roxanne," I corrected automatically while lost in thought.

"Pardon?" he asked bewildered.

And then came the freak-out. I sputtered out in shock, "I don't know you! I can't live with you! And if you're going to offer a random stranger a job and a room in your home, you should at least call her by her name. Mine is Roxanne."

"Serious as shit, I'm giving you a way out, and you want to give me shit over what I call you? My brother lives there too, so you won't be stuck alone with me, at least not always. Though he's a trucker, so he's gone a fair bit. Now, are you getting behind the counter or what?"

"Dude, do you even see what I'm wearing? This is not the proper office attire. Like, at all." I gestured to my amazingly horrible laundry day clothes.

"Don't call me dude and I don't give a rat's ass what you're wearing, so do you want the job or not?" He was getting impatient, but I couldn't stop myself from prodding him.

"Well, I mean, yeah, of course, I do. But I didn't even brush my hair today, and this is my laundry-day outfit. And earlier I was wearing my PJs, so what if this is all I own? Have you thought about that?"

"I don't give a shit. You'll be working the front counter at a garage; it ain't like you'll be entertaining the pope or having to get under a hood. Wear what you want as long as you get the job done, and you're decent. Besides, you got some kick-ass legs."

"Can I take the job and just keep my, uh, other accommodations?"

"You can, but pay's shit, Sweetness. Doubt it will keep you in kibble, fix your car, and pay for a room for more than a couple days."

I had no clue why I was arguing with this man. It was a knee jerk reaction, and I couldn't seem to stop needling him. "So, what you're saying is that you will give me a job, expect good work, and only pay subpar wages?"

"I haven't even told you what you would be making, and you're already giving me shit. I would think you would at least get your first check before you started bitching about a raise."

His words were harsh, but his tone was partly exasperated, mostly amused. I couldn't help but smile at the way he said it. He was right. I stumbled into town, and he saved me on the side of the road, made sure I made it to safety, and then offered to fix my car, give me a job, and offered me a place to stay all within hours of meeting me, so really, I could be a little more grateful about everything. I made a kissy noise at my boy and issued a verbal command saying, "Come on, Zeusyboy. Mommy has some paperwork to fill out."

When I looked back at Jinx, I saw his lips curved up in a smile, and after staring at my ass for a second, he shook his head and fell in line to go to the office to get me the paperwork. He still carried my keys, one of the rings around his pointer finger and the big hot-pink fuzzy Victoria's Secret ball keychain swinging around in circles as he walked.

CHAPTER THREE

Roxanne

After a quick conversation, we decided that I would start the next day, so I filled out the application and handed it over to an amused Jinx. I had Zeus lie down behind the counter, then followed Jinx out to the car and watched as he popped the hood and fiddled with some things.

After a few moments of tinkering, he had one of the other guys—an old man wearing grease-stained coveralls, a bandana wrapped around his head keeping his long shaggy, gray hair out of his eyes, and a weary and weathered look to him—pull my car into the bay before they lifted it on some sort of elevator thing and poked and prodded at it with random tools. I tried to watch in interest, but I was bored to the gills because this was not my thing. Finally, they lowered my car, and the old guy, whom Jinx called Pops—and really I hoped he wasn't his Dad because, who names their kid Jinx anyways—backed my car out of the bay and parked it in a spot outside the garage before he came back in, tossing my keys to Jinx and disappearing behind another car.

Jinx wiped his hands on the mostly black but used-to-be-red rag and pushed it back into his back pocket as he made his way toward me. "Definitely your fuel pump, and you could use a tune-up and new tires."

Ugh. Of course, there would be more than one thing wrong with my car. I knew I was lucky to have made it as far as I had without having any work done to it after all the traveling we'd done over the last year and a half. "Ok, so how much is all of this going to cost me?"

"You workin' here means you get it at cost. You decide to stay with me, where I know you're safe, then you can have it without labor. We can square up by you working here when we're open and helping me with what you can."

"Wait, so you are paying me to work here and still cutting me a deal on the parts and labor?"

"However you want to look at it, just as long as you see things my way."

"What if I were an ax murderer? I mean, I did promise you my first kid. Doesn't that strike you as a little loony tunes?"

"Sweetness, will you just take a little kindness when it's thrown your way? I don't want anything out of you but what I said, so what's the holdup?"

I could tell he was serious this time, so I took a moment to consider what he was saying.

I just couldn't understand what would make someone so willing to take another person in and trust them with a family member and all of their belongings while giving them a leg up. I mean, by all rights, he could have driven past me on the side of the road and not looked back, and I wouldn't have expected any differently. But instead, he was giving me a job, helping me with my car, and offering me a place to stay with a dog I could tell he wasn't altogether sure about.

I wasn't used to this kind of thoughtfulness from anyone and wasn't sure how to take it. I think he could tell my hesitation, because he spoke again, saying gruffly, "Baby, seriously, you get on your feet or decide it's time to move on, you're free to go. I won't ask anything of you except that you give us a heads-up, so we can get someone else into man the office, because serious as shit, I hate being cooped up in there, and so do all of the boys."

I'd spent my whole life not making connections and not owing anyone anything, but this tanned man with long black hair pulled back in a bun that should have looked ridiculous but for some reason only made him look better, lots of facial hair and tattoos covering what seemed like every inch of his body made me want to take a chance and reach out to another human being for once in my life. I tested him; I couldn't seem to help it. "I'm good for a few days, so can we revisit the subject of where I sleep later?"

He smiled in a way that softened his rough edges and took years off his face when he said, "Ok. You take the day to sort your shit and be here tomorrow morning at seven-thirty. I'll have Pops or one of the boys give you a rundown of the office and how everything works, and I'll let you sit on making a decision on staying at mine for a few days."

"Ok," I accepted begrudgingly.

"Wednesday, I'll be on my bike, and I'll come pick you up, so we can hit the compound for a few drinks, and you can get to know the other brothers who will more than likely be coming through here."

"Compound?" My nose wrinkled as I tested the word on my tongue. "That sounds... ominous."

"Compound." He confirmed, "It's an old factory that was shut down decades ago. The MC bought it and renovated it so we'd have a place to call home. Some of the brothers live there, or on the property. And it's the place where we meet up to discuss business and have get-togethers."

"So, it's like a halfway house for bikers?"

His lip quirked up on one side, and he shook his head but didn't respond. I took that as an affirmative and let it go. It was time to call it a day. I didn't speak as I rounded him and got Zeus to hop into the car. When he was loaded up, and I was about to duck into the driver's seat, I heard a sharp whistle ring out and looked up to see Jinx give a lazy salute and turn on his heel to walk back into the car bay.

I climbed in and breathed a sigh of relief when Sally started up with no problems. I swung in to get a pizza from the take-out place and drove to the end of the island where there was an open stretch of beach. We were calling it a night, even though it was still early in the afternoon and I had a whole city at my hands to discover. All I had the energy to do was wash one of my nicer outfits in the sink of the bathroom of a gas station with bars on the windows, then take them out to the car. After driving to the beach, I laid them across the hood to hopefully air dry before morning and called it an early night.

I took my guy for a walk before bed and didn't get a single side-glance from anyone we passed. People were funny in the reactions they had to a pitbull, so I was relieved when he wasn't eyed like a ticking time bomb.

It suddenly occurred to me that Jinx may expect me to leave my dog in the room I supposedly had all day tomorrow, but quickly I decided that if he did, he would have said so, so I rolled my windows down just a little to let the breeze coming off the water blow into my car. Then I locked the doors before grabbing the blanket from the passenger seat and bringing it up to rest my head on as a makeshift pillow. I was still wearing my ratty laundry-day outfit as I was lulled to sleep by the snores coming from my backseat. I decided as I drifted off that all in all, it had been a good day, and I'd be damned if I questioned it further. Tomorrow would bring whatever it brought, but today had been one of my better days, and I was feeling cautiously optimistic for my immediate future.

CHAPTER FOUR

Jinx

Pops was leaning against the wall when I turned back toward the garage bay that the Mustang had just filled. I knew the old bastard was going to voice his opinion on something; he felt like that was his right as one of the founding member of the Mischief Makers MC and my deceased dad's best friend.

Pops, Wide Load, Polar Bear, and my dad, Big 'Un, founded this MC straight out of 'Nam. A giant fuck-you to the establishment in general, they liked to say; but while a lot of clubs claimed they were about family, we truly were.

Scratch, my best friend, the club's sergeant at arms and the offspring of Wide Load and his old lady, Birdie, my brother, Nomad, and I had all grown up on the compound, in the life; Rammer and Jammer, the annoying twins who belonged to Polar Bear, were doing the required stint as prospects before they could claim their patches and officially join the brotherhood, but there were no doubts that it would happen.

We were legacy, and we had each served our country.

A few of the brothers had come in during my old man's stint as prez, Q Ball, my VP, and Freight Train, my Road Captain being two of them. Turn-Pike, Mouse, and more recently, Tadpole had come in under my gavel, and Gunny was a newer member of our chapter but had been a part of the Bayview Chapter after coming home from the first wave of troops to hit the desert in the Middle East after 9/11.

We'd all done our time.

We were a Motorcycle Club of Veterans doing our best to keep the island we lived on clean while being relatively law-abiding citizens. The last thing I had time for was a distraction that had legs that looked the way Roxanne's did, nine kinds of problems I was itching to solve, and a history that I wanted to know everything about.

I shook out a smoke and lit it, then lifted an eyebrow, waiting. The old man wheezed away from the wall and spat to the left before gesturing his head in the direction where I had left her. "Bitch is trouble."

I didn't fully understand his tone, but his words pissed me off, which shifted me out of my lazy stance. Shoulders straightened and face set, I dared, "Come again?"

He watched me for a few moments, and I tried to discern the look on his face as he searched mine but decided the bastard was going 'round the bend when he threw back his head and laughed his raspy smoker's laugh, tar-stained teeth showing and scraggly and ridiculously long, mostly gray beard shaking. He laughed until he had to wipe tears from the creases of his eyes. I just watched.

Hell, maybe this was what an old, rusted-out biker looked like when he'd finally cracked. I was debating punching the fucker just to shut him up, but he finally got himself under control and said, "About got'am time, boy."

So, maybe he had lost it. I asked, "What the fuck you

ramblin' about, Pops?" instead of hitting him, just to be on the safe side.

"Heard you trying to get her to shack up with you and wanted to see which way the wind was blowing. Didn't know if you were itchin' for a house mouse or an ol' lady."

Such was the fine line that I walked. As I was his president, he shouldn't be pushing this shit, but I was also one of the boys he'd stood in for as a father figure, he felt it was his place to poke at every damn thing.

"The wind is blowing like a woman with no family and nowhere to go rolled onto the island that we claim as ours, and I'm trying to make sure the fuckin' Bangers don't get 'hold of her. What the hell do you think they would do with a girl like her?"

"Well, fuck me, brother. I didn't know we were running a halfway house for any homeless single bitches that hit our territory. My apologies."

That one pissed me off. "We got a problem? Last I checked, it wasn't anyone else's business if I offer a bitch a room or not."

"So, she is a bitch, then?"

He was fucking with me.

That was when I realized it. I shook my head and walked away muttering, "Stupid fucking old man."

He laughed again as I hit the door to the office, so I flipped him the bird and slammed the door in his face.

CHAPTER FIVE

Roxanne

To say that working at the shop every day was a natural transition would be sugarcoating it a lot, but on my first day, with Zeus in tow, I was introduced to everyone who worked in the shop. To my surprise, most of these guys were rough around the edges and tattooed to the max, but as a whole, they were all fairly polite.

I arrived at Double M at 7:45 and found the lot deserted, so I sat in my seat, mentally pep-talking myself into believing that this could somehow be a good idea. I was so deep in thought that when the roar of motorcycle pipes finally cracked my thoughts, I jumped and let out a ridiculous little yelp in alarm. Then I watched in fascination as five very impressive-looking motorcycles and what appeared to be a fancy motorized reverse tricycle filed behind the building. What struck me the most was that every single man on a bike was wearing matching leather vests with some matching designs on the back.

They looked like it was Twinkie-Tuesday at the biker auto repair shop.

After introductions were made all around—and really,

these guys were determined to call me anything but my actual name, because with the little bit of background Jinx had given them on me, I'd been dubbed Gypsy; although frustratingly, Jinx stuck with calling me Sweetness—Jinx had Pops walk me through the front office procedures. Mostly, there was nothing to do but secretarial and bookkeeping work, so I was ok with that. Zeus and I settled in for a long day behind the counter.

Surprisingly, after a few hours, Jinx came in, let out a whistle, and patted his leg, drawing my dog's attention. Then he walked right back through the doors to the garage bays with Zeus trailing him.

Stupefied, I stood there for a moment in shock before deciding to follow them out to see what the hell.

"Jinx? What the heck?"

He looked at me and winked before walking through a door at the back of the shop.

Well, there was no way he was getting away with that for one more second, so I marched my tail right out the door behind him and was shocked all over again as I watched him open the door to a huge pickup truck and motion for my dog to get in.

What. The. Hell.

"Just what in the heck do you think you're doing?"

"Figured I got the monster in my truck, you would follow, and we could get out of here and grab a bite to eat. I didn't intend for you to hide behind the counter the whole day. You can wander around. Someone comes in; they ring the bell or one of the brothers hollers for you."

I found myself climbing into the truck even as I said, "I'm really not hungry, and besides, I've never really had a job like this, so it's kinda fun to just sit back there and chat with people as they come in."

"Sweetness, most of the people you've dealt with so far today have been on the phone, and of the five people you have seen face-to-face, you've spent the majority of the time talking to Pops, and he's supposed to be working, not flirting with the staff."

I snorted and replied, "Am I correct in saying that you said this morning, and I quote, 'Old man, show her the ropes. I fuckin' hate paperwork' before disappearing for the next few hours?"

He reached out and playfully tugged a tendril of my hair that had slipped from my tie and responded, "You went to college, so you obviously know how to work a computer. Walking you through the basics should have taken a half-hour tops, yet when I walked in there an hour ago, I heard the two of you discussing commands in German and debating which of your breeds were the better dogs, his Chihuahuas or your Pit."

While I cringed and mentally thought *buuuuuuusted*, verbally, all I said was, "Well, obviously, Pits are the better breed. We *all* know that Chihuahuas are evil little fuckers!"

He snorted back a laugh and put his right hand on the wheel, using his left to tap along to some unheard beat while shaking his head.

I realized he did that a lot around me and I found myself smiling for no real reason as the wind blew through the open windows, and I sat beside a man I had met only days before and already felt connected to. My boy had his tongue hanging out in a big Pitbull grin, just enjoying the ride.

It struck me that I had never been content just to be. I

wasn't running from anything, and I had no fears. No worries were clouding my mind, and I was riding in a tow truck with my boy and a gorgeous man who seemed intent on changing my wandering ways while I annoyed him just because I could.

"Where are we going?"

"Mama's," he grunted at me.

I froze in terror.

Oh no. Oh, hell no.

"I am not going to your *mother's* house!" I shrieked.

He made a choking sound and shook his head but didn't have time to respond before he was pulling into the parking lot of a café with the word 'Mama's' emblazoned on the sign by the road.

Oh.

Whew.

"There's a restaurant called Mama's? That's weird; you know that, right? And what about my guy?"

"He can come, too. We'll sit outside. One of the girls will come out and take our orders."

Jinx shut off the engine, climbed out of the truck, and made his way around to my side as I opened the door and jumped to the ground. I patted my leg, and Zeus bounded out of the cab. I saw as we walked around the side of the restaurant that there was a covered patio with picnic tables and torches, setting the scene for a rustic outing.

I sat across from Jinx, and Zeus lay down on the ground at the end of the table. As he sat, he adjusted his vest and rested an elbow on the picnic table. The at-ease posture he held himself in relaxed me enough that I could ask him, "Why do you guys all have matching vests?"

He looked at me for a moment in silent shock and then spoke. "Our cuts? Sweetness, you remember me telling you about the club? We, the brothers at the shop, a few others, and I are part of a motorcycle club called the Mischief Makers. We all have our cuts, the vests, and wear them all the time because we're proud of our brotherhood and have busted ass to earn the patches we have on them."

"It just seems so silly. Like, you all have matching 'cuts'? You and your 'brothers'? Those guys aren't all your brothers; they can't be. Half of them are old enough to be your dad."

His eyes twinkled at my naivete, and he said, "Quit thinking quite as literal as you are. These guys all have histories. And no, they aren't my biological brothers, but the bond we have is thicker than most have with their blood kin; though incidentally, my actual brother is a brother in the club as well. We choose to be a part of this family and bust our asses to earn our spot. It's almost like a corporation within a family. The shop is part of the club's holdings, as is the towing business, the strip club, the bar, and a few other ventures. We work together and make a comfortable living. We aren't blood. We're a hell of a lot closer than that."

He was talking about family and business, but I was stuck on the fact that they owned a strip club. A strip club! "You guys own a strip club?"

"Yeah, Sweetness, among other things. Why? You dance?"

"I'm sorry?" I shrieked *a-freaking-gain*.

"Do you dance?"

"As in strip?" I swear my face went up in flames. I mean, did I look like a dancer? I didn't even wear heels!

"So, no?" The bastard smirked.

"What the hell, dude? Why would you think I was a stripper? I mean, yeah, I can dress like a hoochie mama when the mood strikes, but I've never taken my clothes off for any man except for my ex. Ugh. Even my dog isn't allowed in the room when I'm naked." I was such a prude.

He roared with laughter as the waitress walked up. She was in her mid-thirties, tops, and had an unidentifiable number of necklaces around her throat all tangled together. She wore fake lashes that looked to be a part of a costume, they were so long, and her makeup was dramatic with bright-red painted lips, fingernails long and black, and rings on each finger with an additional ring on the knuckles of a couple of fingers on both hands. She had bright pink hair that was pulled up into a bun, and a soft smile played at her lips as she approached us.

"How're you two doing?" Her attire and style may have said 'gothic meets pin-up,' but her voice was straight sweet Texas twang. I struggled not to fidget in my seat when her eyes came to me, and her smile went luminous. "Dante, who is this? I haven't seen her before!" Before I could process who in the heck Dante was, she thrust her hand in my direction and introduced herself. "Hey, girl, I'm Maisie! I haven't seen you around the clubhouse, and you sure don't look like the usual morning after sperm receptacle. Dante, where did you find her?"

The tentative smile that had begun to spread across my lips faltered as I watched Jinx's body go tight and heard him mutter, "Fuck."

Louder, he said, "Jesus fuck, Maisie, you don't even think before you open your mouth, do you?" But rather than angry, he sounded almost resigned.

"Maisie, Roxanne. Roxanne, Maisie."

When he said my name, I couldn't decide if it would be weird of me to reach out a hand to shake but didn't have to choose when Maisie suddenly grabbed my hand and patted it while saying, "Roxanne! Oh, I feel all kinds of vibes coming from your aura! Girl, you need to let me do a reading for you! I am feeling all the juju. Let me go grab a couple of menus and bring y'all some water!"

Maisie pranced away in a whirlwind, which was pretty much how I would describe her from start to finish. I felt like I had just been picked up by a tornado, spun around a few times, and then tossed back into my seat. Just from that short interaction, I had so many questions I didn't even know where to start. I just sat, staring at Jinx with my jaw hanging open.

A resigned look came over his face, and I swear he muttered, "Fuckin' Maisie," and while I could have been wrong; but somehow I didn't think I was. "I'm guessing there is a lot there that needs covering, but I gotta be real honest and say that I would rather not talk about any of it here."

I thought about it for a moment before I spoke, "Well, I think I caught the majority of what she said. I don't look like your usual bed partner, she may be batshit crazy, and your real name isn't Jinx, which explains a lot, since that is such an odd name, and I couldn't figure that one out."

He laughed out loud at that but said no more, so I let it go and instead looked around, just taking everything in.

I felt that warmth in my chest again, and it was a feeling so nice that I knew that no matter where life took me next, I'd always look back on this day and smile.

CHAPTER SIX

Roxanne

I didn't have a schedule that I was aware of, and it was way past five, but the guys were still in the shop working, so I took the time to clean up. I'd just finished scrubbing the bathrooms, and *eww* that was a horrifying experience, when Jinx walked in and did a double-take when he saw me. "Sweetness, you could have cut out of here two hours ago. When we shut the bay doors, we're closed for business, and your day is done."

"Okay, I wasn't sure, and to be honest, the place needed a good scrubbing, but I'll close up and get out of here now."

"Alright. Before I forget, heads-up! See ya in the morning." I scrambled to catch the keys and didn't bother to say good-bye as I marveled at them because if I wasn't mistaken, the man had just given me the keys to the garage, and there were a few other keys on there as well. I didn't understand the instant trust in me but whatever.

I patted my leg and got Zeus to get up and follow me to the door. It'd been a long day, and I was wiped. We still had to find something to eat, and I needed to scrub another top, at the very least, that I could wear tomorrow.

Dollar taco night was a winner for us, and I decided to

treat myself and use some of the carefully stashed away cash I had leftover from waiting tables in Texarkana for two months, at the laundromat so I could wash my clothes in an actual machine while we ate our tacos.

After I finished eating, I put the clothes in the dryer and took Zeus out for a walk. He took care of his business, and we had the laundry loaded back up and on the way to our trusty parking spot on the beach with the top down. It was a beautiful night, and there were worse places to be.

Like Seattle. It may be where I was from, but it wasn't home. I'd never had that.

After another walk, the sun had set, and the constant breeze coming in from the ocean gave me as close to a feeling of home, whatever that was, as I'd ever felt. I could hear bike pipes in the distance and vaguely wondered if it was one of the brothers. Thankfully, I wasn't visible from the road. I'd charged my phone in the office that day, so I pulled it out of the glove box to check my email. That is, until I realized that I had over two thousand of them. I tossed it back in the glove box with a sigh and leaned back in my seat. Zeus laid a paw on my leg over the center console, but that was the extent of our activity as the roar of motorcycle pipes continued getting closer and closer.

Finally, the three-wheeled bike that Pops rode pulled into the parking area beside me, and the engine died. The long-haired, tattooed, old man climbed off and walked over to my car. I straightened and waited to see what he would say.

As far as they knew, I was staying at the motel, so I was sticking with that story. That didn't stop my heart from feeling as if it were about to pound right out of my chest, though.

He walked around my car and leaned a hip on the passenger door, bending over to scratch Zeus on the hindquarter. "Whatcha doin' out here this late, Gypsygirl?"

I answered him as honestly as I could, "Taking a moment to be. They're so rare that when I can find one, I take it."

He was watching me, looking for a tell, a sign of deception, but I was sure that he didn't know me well enough to notice the way I suddenly needed to touch my middle finger to my thumb and tap. His attention was on my face. The need to tap those fingers together was almost overwhelming. It wouldn't be long before a cold sweat broke out over my body. "I hear that. You 'bout ready to call it a night? Not real safe out here for you."

That kinda pissed me off, especially with me so wound up, so I asked in a nasty voice, "Oh yeah?"

He just watched me in what I was realizing was just his way before one corner of his lips tipped up, and he replied, "Yeah. Now I know you carry a weapon, and that's great. Know you got this hellhound of yours, and that's mighty fine as well, but we got some riffraff out here. Don't want you getting tied up in anything, especially with your affiliation to the club."

"Well, no worries. We're going to be calling it a night soon and heading back to our room. Thanks for the concern, Pops, but we're gonna be okay, and we'll be there in the morning with bells on." Could he just go already?

He looked like he was going to say something further and I sucked in a breath as I waited, but he let it go and instead smiled and patted the car door before walking back around to get to his bike. Now I felt like a jerk, so I spoke up, "Pops?"

He turned around to look back at me. "Gypsy?"

"Sorry. Thanks for worrying. I'm not used to it. Haven't had anyone who cared, well, ever, so it takes some getting used to."

The stiffness went out of his posture, and he quirked a soft smile at me and climbed onto his bike.

He was long gone when I realized that I was still on edge, and his words had done their job. I was scared in a way that I hadn't been before. The peacefulness of the moment was gone, and now all I wanted to do was close the convertible roof and secure myself in the car before taking my gun out and making sure I had a bullet chambered and the safety locked.

I spent the rest of the night uneasy in my driver's seat, barely sleeping a wink.

CHAPTER SEVEN

Roxanne

I was dragging, and it was apparent to everyone around.

I hadn't slept much at all last night, and I was paying for it today. I stayed on top of my work and got everything done, but I knew it was obvious that something was wrong, and the looks I was getting from Pops let me know that maybe I hadn't pulled the wool over his eyes after all. He was watching me more than usual. It didn't seem like he'd said anything to Jinx or Scratch yet, but I couldn't be sure, so I was skittish around all of them all day.

After the bay doors were closed, I went ahead and locked the front door and tried to sneak out. After all, today was the day; the day when I would be going to the compound to meet all the brothers, which just seemed really overwhelming.

And since I'd already decided that I would be leaving town as soon as I could get my car fixed and pay Jinx back, there was no reason to throw my lot in with them. I would be here and gone before they knew it.

I almost made it to my car when the whistle drew my attention back, and I saw Jinx standing there waiting for me. "Yo, Sweetness, you're with me."

"Jinx, I can't leave Zeus here, and he can't ride on your bike. We'll follow you in my car. Plus, that way we can leave as soon as we're ready, and you won't have to leave the party. I've heard Scratch say three different times today that this could get crazy. Safety first!" I tried to smile believably, but even I could hear the desperation in my voice.

He watched me for a second in hooded regard and then nodded in agreement. "Right, you follow Pops to the compound, and he'll get you a drink. The boys and I will be right behind you."

I could handle that, so I nodded and smiled. "Awesome!"

Jinx shook his head. It was his signature move, especially when I did something especially silly, like shouting, 'Awesome!'

It was interesting pulling onto the compound for the first time. There was a really tall chain-link fence surrounding the property, and two guys who had to be the twins and were wearing a less ornamented version of the other guys' cuts pushed each side of the gate back until we pulled through. Once we were clear, they closed the doors again and remained there on lookout. Pops parked next to a building that didn't appear to have any windows, so I pulled up between him and one of the tow trucks belonging to the shop. I pulled the leash that we rarely used out of the console and clipped it to Zeus' collar. He didn't need a leash to walk, but I wasn't sure what we were walking into, so this seemed like the best alternative.

I beeped the lock on my car and immediately felt foolish because I was locked in, and the way the guys I could see looked, if they wanted in my car, they would go straight for the window anyways.

Pops held open a thick, solid steel door, and we stepped into a vast room. At one end, there was a huge television showing a boxing match, and there were three couches spread out, one of them holding a very large-bodied man at one end and a super slim one at the other, both of whom looked to be around Pops' age. A handful of chairs, ranging from barstools to camp chairs, a recliner, and even a couple of bean bags were spread out. The other end of the room had a restaurant-sized bar with mirrored walls and dozens of bottles and at least ten more barstools. Spread through the middle of the room were a pool table, an air hockey table, and another couch.

Before I could decide where I wanted to look first, Pops tapped my arm and led me to the bar. "What'll it be, Gypsy?"

My plan was to make the quickest escape that I could, so I requested, "Just a Coke, please?" and took a seat on one of the stools at the bar.

He walked behind the bar and grabbed a Solo cup from a cabinet, then plopped a bit of ice, from somewhere under the bar, into it and handed me the cup of ice and a can of soda before grabbing himself a beer and pulling up a stool to sit across from me.

Well, this isn't awkward.

It was almost like he picked up that particular thought because he was grinning when my eyes hit him and shaking his head. "I like you, girl. You've got a fire in you, very much like my Louisa did. I think you're going to do just fine."

That gave me pause. "What do you mean, I'll do just fine?"

He regarded my face for a moment and said, "Something between you and the boy. I can see it all over the two of you.

You're a scrapper, so I imagine that something is gonna start to weigh on you, and you're gonna want to run. Gotta know, a lot is going on here. Times are dangerous. But you stick with us, and Jinx will see it to the other side. There's a reason a grizzled old bastard like me will follow a man like him. You're gonna see that and be glad you stuck, I suspect."

We had to be having two different conversations because nothing he was saying made any sense. "Uh, Pops, this is just a stop on the map for me. I'm not looking to settle down or stick around long term."

He smiled at me. Whatever that meant. I didn't have to contemplate it anymore because I could hear the roar of multiple bikes and figured it was a safe assumption that the cavalry had arrived. Pops stood and moved the barstool he'd been sitting on back out of the way and reached down to pull out several beers as men walked in talking loudly.

Zeus looked up at the approaching men and then, giving his head a shake and jingling his collar, he laid it back down and immediately started snoring again. That caused Scratch to snort. "Look at him acting all innocent, like the fucker wouldn't eat one of us just to see what we taste like."

A couple of the other guys guffawed or snorted, but my protection of Zeus was already well known, and Jinx wasn't the only one who kept needling me. "Don't be jealous that the dog looks better than you, brother. You have one of those faces that only a mother can love," one of the other guys picked at him.

I smiled at that but stayed quiet. Jinx hadn't come in with them, and I was waiting on him to show up so I could see all of them with a beer in hand, then get the hell out of here. The guys each grabbed one and nodded their thanks to Pops before walking across the room to a thick wooden door. I noticed that there was a hand-drawn replica of their club logo, the eerily smiling skull with a heart and spade as eyes, an upside-down club as his nose, and a jester's hat with the points, which had a diamond with the number 13 on one end, a skull and crossbones on a second, and an eight ball on the third. Before each man walked into the room, he did some kind of one-handed chest tap and then reached out and touched the logo. It looked as if they were paying homage to it.

When only Pops, Scratch, and I remained, the two other men across the room got up and ambled their way over to us and took a seat. More beers came out, and the skinny man, Polar Bear, growled, "And Jinx?"

Pops angled his head toward me, which I pretended to ignore even though I wanted to know where he was as well. "Business. He'll be here in five."

The fat man grunted and said, "Would that his jackass brother got his ass back home where he belongs, the brother wouldn't have so much on his shoulders and might be able to enjoy life's little"—he jerked his head in my direction—"luxuries."

I watched Pops bite his lips to hold back a laugh as I sat there, stunned. I mean, how often did a girl get referred to as a luxury anyways? These guys were mental.

I jumped in surprise when the door to the outside jerked open again, and this time the man himself swaggered in. "Bitches are here."

Wait. What?

I couldn't stop it from pouring out of my mouth. "Did he

just say-"

This time, Pops laughed out loud while I gaped.

Jinx walked in like he had missed the whole exchange even though I could see that he was fighting a smile, and said, "Got church, Sweetness. Gimme about twenty minutes, and I'll introduce you around."

And with that, the men who had been loitering around the bar with me all grabbed their beers, did that chest tap-wall tap thing to the drawing, and walked out of the room. Jinx was next to last with Scratch bringing up the rear and shutting the door behind him, but not before giving me a wink.

"Well, that wasn't weird or anything, was it, buddy?" I asked my dog since he was the only living thing in my vicinity.

That didn't stay true, though. I heard at least two women walking up, giggling, and watched them walk through the heavy door like they'd done it a million times. Right, these must be the 'bitches' he'd been referring to.

The girls finally caught sight of me and slowed down momentarily before coming to the bar.

One of the women, a particularly busty one who had a breathiness to her voice that some women seemed to think men liked, even though it made them sound ridiculous, remarked, "Haven't seen you around here before. Who do you belong to?"

"Belong to?"

"Yeah. Which brother do you belong to?"

"Uhh, none of them? I work at the shop."

"What's with the giant dog? Is he going to bite?" This was the higher-pitched voice of Busty Girl's friend.

I was offended by that, so I snapped, "Absolutely not!"

The girls eyed me for a few more moments and then looked at each other, and I watched as they decided that I was clearly not competition. I sipped on my already flat and warm soda and waited for the guys to finish up whatever they were doing, so I could make a graceful exit and get out of here. The two women, Denette and Suzanne, as I'd learned by listening to their conversation, were driving me batshit crazy.

Their voices and the ridiculousness of the conversations, gossip about the women the brothers slept with combined with the thinly veiled insults aimed my way, were enough to make any person snap. But I bit my tongue because I didn't know who they were and I was the outsider here.

Finally, even Zeus was getting tired of hanging around doing nothing, and he started to get annoying, trying to jump on my lap to get my attention or licking at his no-longer-there balls really loudly. My head was going to explode soon.

I looked at my watch and realized that it had been almost an hour, not the promised twenty minutes, so I got up and said, "Will y'all let Jinx know that I'm heading back to my room now? I'll see them at work tomorrow."

Busty Girl waved me off while she continued listening to her friend, so I crossed the room and walked out to my car. Zeus was eager to hit the road, so he jumped in and settled down. I drove to the gate, where one of the twins walked to my driver's side window, so I rolled it down and smiled, waiting.

"You goin' already, babe? Party can't even really be going yet."

I pretended to be one with the natives, as it were, and said, "The boys are still in church, and it's getting past our bedtime. We have to get back to our room so we can call it a night.

Gotta be at work bright and early in the morning." I wasn't sure my terminology was right but sighed with relief when he seemed to accept it.

"Alright, I hear ya. Be safe!" He patted the lip of my door and then ran to the front to push one side of the fence back so that I could squeeze through.

I didn't notice a tail.

I'd let my guard down, and even though I was vaguely annoyed about the way my evening had turned out, I wasn't looking out for trouble. I should've been, but I wasn't. And since I wasn't, it was a shock when it found me instead.

CHAPTER EIGHT

Jinx

I was fucking pissed.

I'd walked in for church, handled business, although it admittedly took longer than I'd planned, and walked out to find Roxanne and show her around only to realize she had left.

An hour ago.

One of the bitches who regularly showed up at the club when they knew there was a party going down had told me at first that she must have gone to the bathroom, but she still hadn't come out half an hour later. We figured out she'd left when Pops, the dirty bastard, walked out of the bathroom with the big-tittied bitch who came with her.

I pulled him aside to see if she'd said anything to him and was surprised when he cut me off and started cussing. "Fuck, I knew I forgot some-damn-thing. Yesterday, I was doing a turn around the island and found her parked out on the pub beach. Looked like she had plans to stay there. Just how sure are you that our girl has a place to stay?"

That set me back a step. "Are you telling me she may be shacking up in her car on the beach, the beach that the Bangers have been trying to take over for months, and you didn't think to say anything?"

Scratch walked up and rested an elbow on my shoulder, not in the affectionate way that it looked but to remind his prez and best friend to get a lock on it. I took a moment and then said, "Right, well, there's only one way to know for sure. Load up, you two. Let's take a ride. We're either about to drag her ass back here or wake her up in her hotel room and find out why she left the party early." Pops grinned and turned on his heel and Scratch chuckled and dropped his arm to follow.

At the gate, the twins rushed out to open the door and let us through, and Pops and Scratch fell in side by side behind me as we gunned it and with throttles wide open, roared to the public access beach.

I was cursing before we even got across the parking lot. Not only was she there, but two of the Bangers were as well, and she had them at gunpoint while that monster of hers was holding himself tight, ready to attack and kill for his mistress if needed. It pissed me off, even more, when I realized that these were two Bangers I'd never seen before. The street gang with deep ties to the cartel had been funneling drugs and thugs onto the island for months, and even though I knew those tats, I hadn't seen these two before.

Mother. Fucker.

Instead of letting any of that show on my face, I cut the motor, swung off my bike, and waited as my brothers did the same. I strolled over like I wasn't about to kill someone with my bare hands, which was a definite possibility.

"Seems like the Bangers have been told to stay off this part of the island. Didn't we sit down with Vincent himself not even six weeks ago, brother?" I asked Scratch, even though I knew we had.

"Shit, brother, seems like you even warned them that the next Bangers found on Double M territory might end up going back over the border in a body bag."

Pops spat and then said, "Back in my day, we would've already killed the fuckers. You ladies wanna sit here and discuss knitting patterns, too, or can we get back to the club? I got my dick wet, and now I'd appreciate a beer to cool down with. Not dealing with some riffraff street kids tryin' to be gangsters."

One of the guys being forced to stay put while Zeus and Roxanne held them off with their threats cursed and acted like he was going to step forward. I lost the easiness of my posture and snarled, "Obviously, you know she belongs to us, so what the fuck do you think you're doing? Did your boss not warn you that we fight back? And then cut your fucking head off?"

There was no response from my audience. The two being held by weapon and attack dog had just realized that there was a pistol strapped to my leg, and the would-be badass had decided to go mute. "Right. Here's what's going to happen. You two are going to scram, and you're gonna go back to El Jefe and let him know that if I see a Banger on Double M territory again, they're going to be fishing someone out of the Gulf. Sweetness, call him off and let them go. They aren't going to bother you anymore."

I watched her to see if she would do as I said, and it took a moment, but I saw the tension leave her shoulders. She lowered her gun, clicked on the safety, and reached down to pet the tense, extremely pissed-off dog. The monster stayed at attention, but some of the tension left his meaty body with her touch.

The Bangers ran as soon as they saw her distract him, and I told her, "Put him in the fucking car and get your ass back to the compound right now." Thank Christ, she didn't argue and instead nodded and loaded the dog up. I nodded at Scratch to follow her back and lock her down. I was too damn pissed to attempt that myself just yet.

We watched them drive away when Pops laughed. "I called that one. Knew she meant something to you. I see you feel a connection to her. In case you're wondering, she feels it, too. Don't think a woman who has her personality would have quietly gone back to the compound, doing as she's told without having something there. She seems the type to drive the other way just to piss you off."

I ran my hands over my face, scratching at my beard. "What the fuck am I going to do with a woman?"

"Well, son, if your daddy didn't tell you about the birds and the bees, I'm not real sure what you've been doing with all those girls over the years in your room. Y'all playing bridge or somethin'?"

That made me laugh. "Shut the hell up, old man. You know what I mean. She's trouble, and I have more of that than I can handle already."

"So, tell her to pack up and clear off the island when we get back. She's off the island, the Bangers won't fuck with her, and she's out of your hair."

I looked at him at that and saw that he was blowing smoke. There was no way he thought I was going to let her go, and there was no way I was ready to yet either. I wasn't sure what this was between us, but it needed to be explored. As good of an idea as it would be to send her packing, I knew I could keep her safe, and that's what I was going to do. I wouldn't be sending her out there with a drug-dealing ex and nothing to keep her safe but a dog and a gun. Those days were over for her. I pulled my phone out of my pocket and, dialing, I said, "I fucking should. I really fucking should."

"Yeah." Really, what else could he say? That was it. There was nothing else to say about it. I should, but we both knew I wouldn't.

"Yes?" came the voice through the phone at my ear.

"Vincent. Thought we had an agreement? See, I've been coming to these sit-downs with you and Alabama, and it seemed that we were making some headway on getting to the bottom of this bullshit. Yet I find one of my girls getting terrorized on the beach, clearly on our territory. The fuck, man?"

"Ahh, my friend Jinx. See, my boys just called to tell me a completely different story. They told me that a woman who's been on the island only days held them at gunpoint and had her rabid dog on them. Seems to me that part of our agreement centered on you and your people leaving mine alone."

"Now, Vincent, that may be the case, but she's been Double M's since she crossed the I-45 bridge onto our little slice of heaven. And she wasn't threatening them; she was defending herself." I didn't know this for a fact, but I couldn't see any other reason for the situation we'd rolled up on. "I'm telling you all official-like now that the girl belongs to us and she's to be left alone. You or any of your street thugs get a wild hair and want to mess with her, this shit we've been dancing around for months is going to get real really fast."

The other man laughed shortly and then said something that made tendrils of unease uncurl in my stomach. The Beachside Bangers leader spoke, and all traces of civility were gone, "Jinx, shit's already real. And you should probably know, we aren't coming after you boys, but it's open season on Pitbulls and bitches with brass cajones. That comes from above me amigo, and even if I wanted to, I couldn't change it. Lucky for me, I don't."

With that, the other man ended the call, and I felt the rage bubbling up inside me. For months we'd been dancing around a war with the Beachside Bangers and the Cortes Cartel. It was common knowledge that they were using the Bangers to move dope on the island and we'd been going out of our way to inconvenience them every chance we got. Someone ordering a hit on her meant that the gloves were coming off.

"Mother. Fucker," I growled out, and to calm myself and maintain composure, I shook a smoke out and lit it. The cherry burned bright as I inhaled deeply, the smoke searing its way into my lungs. Half the cigarette was gone before I calmed enough to lift my phone and call Scratch.

"Bro?" I could tell from the background noise that he was back on the compound, and involuntarily, the wind went out of me knowing she was safe.

"Scratch, get her and that damn dog and lock them down in my room. Get her keys and grab her shit. She's on the compound, on my bike, or in the office with a brother at all times until I get these motherfuckers on lock."

"Shit. Went that well, did it?"

"Worse. They've put a price on the dog and the girl both

but won't fuck with 'em on Double M or with a brother around. They won't get close, got me?" I didn't let him reply and carried on, "Get Gunny to work the front with Jammer during the week, Rammer on Roxanne anytime she's off the compound with Mouse tailing, if she's not with you, Pops, or me. Daytime, she's on my bike, and that dog is with a brother on Double M."

"10-4, brother. I'm on it." The line went dead after that, and I put the phone back in my pocket, dropped the cigarette to the ground, and made sure it was out with my boot then I nodded at Pops to load back up then we got the hell out of there.

CHAPTER NINE

Roxanne

I was in shock. I'd been on my own for a long time, and that was the first time I had ever had to hold someone at gunpoint. I had just gotten comfortable and was settling in when I heard their voices, and then Zeus started to growl low in his throat in a way I hadn't heard before.

I remember being in Missoula and training Zeus with Zeke, the K-9 trainer I'd met by chance, and thinking about how ridiculous it was to be learning commands that would tell my dog to attack, to act fierce and be ready to attack, to counter all the dog's instincts and instead trust that he would obey my commands only. As soon as I got to a point where I could reach out, I needed to tell Zeke about how perfectly Zeus had handled the situation.

I was pulled out of this reverie when Scratch walked over to me and handed me an ice-cold bottle of water, saying, "Alright, Gypsy, let's get you settled in for the night. Give me your keys, so I can park your car after I take you and killer over there to your room."

I tossed the keys to Scratch, more at his head than his hand, but of course, he caught them by the fuzzy ball keychain.

He shook his head and smirked, though, rather than saying anything about it and led me out of the main area of the clubhouse. I realized just how massive the building was when we passed a hallway that cut to the left and kept walking. We came to a second hallway and turned following it all the way to its end and to a door, which was the only open one, ushering Zeus and me inside.

By the time I realized that this was somebody's bedroom, Scratch, the rat bastard, put a key in the deadbolt and locked the door shut. I couldn't even unlock it because my side had a keyhole as well. It was one of those utterly ridiculous locks that you could only use with the key.

Thankfully, there was a bathroom built-in with this room, so I went to the sink and cupped some water in my hand to splash my face while Zeus climbed onto the bed to get comfortable, a luxury he wasn't accustomed to.

I dried my face and then slipped out of my shoes and lay down on the bed next to my snoring dog. That's how Jinx found me when he unlocked the door and stormed in about a half-hour later.

"What the hell was that, Roxanne?"

I jerked to attention and sat up. Even Zeus was awake and paying attention now. "What?" There was no finishing that thought, though, because he ripped his shirt over his head and yelled loud enough to get a cautious woof from Zeus.

"Are you fucking stupid? You could have been killed!"

The argument I'd prepped myself to give died on my tongue, and I just stared at him. Holy hot dude. In my sleepy state, all that registered was that there were yummy tattooed abs in the same room with a bed... And me.

"Those're the bad guys. Since the Beachside Bangers started getting active in this part of the state, crime rates have skyrocketed, the use of meth and coke has at least tripled, and the people who piss these guys off and don't have the privilege of wearing a cut end up dead!" He kicked off his boots and reached for his belt.

Okay, clearly, this was bigger than I'd realized and I needed to focus.

He dropped the pants and stepped out of them, my focus disappeared quicker than a cheetah chasing a gazelle, and I was almost drooling when he turned and walked to the closet and pulled out a clean outfit wearing only his boxers. Not toward me.

It hit me that he'd still been in his dirty work clothes, so maybe the striptease hadn't been for my benefit.

Even though I'd definitely benefitted.

Perhaps it was time for me to cut my losses and get the hell off this island and out of this state while I was at it. Before I did anything stupid. Or say, cheetah-like. Because pouncing hadn't been out of the question moments before. "Look, Jinx, if you can get us off the island, I'll get out of the state and never look back. No harm, no foul."

"Yeah. Except for the fact that I threw down with a fucking drug cartel to keep you safe. Sure. You just take off and blow the place. Except, no, the hell you are not."

I sat there, perplexed, and trying to understand him. I couldn't understand our situation. I wasn't sure that I'd ever seen someone react with this much passion in, if I was reading this right, my defense. It was crazy.

I was a nowhere girl. No one cared enough to get

invested in my life, and yet this scruffy, angry, scary-looking, potentially outlaw biker had taken up for me and was mad as all hell that I was considering running. "I don't... understand." It was the best I could do to sum up my feelings.

He studied my face intently and then relaxed and barked out a disbelieving laugh before scraping his hands down his face. "Fuckin' hell, Sweetness. I rolled up there and spotted the signs that they were Bangers and damn near swallowed my tongue. You were holding them calm as you please, not a worry in the world, and that dog ready to rip the face off anyone who didn't feel like listening to you. Craziest shit I've ever seen."

"So, they were bad guys?"

"The absolute worst. If you can think it, they've done it or considered it and realized it wouldn't give them enough of a payout and discarded the idea. But make no mistake; there is no kindness or warmth in these guys."

I sat on the edge of the bed, and he came and sat down next to me and grabbed my hand, holding it tightly in his own, thankfully mostly clothed again. "I've gotta go brief my brothers on what's happened, but I need to make sure we're clear on a few things first. You cannot leave the compound unless you're on my bike. The dog can't leave at all." He saw my protest coming and cut me off, "Rox, they've declared open season on you and your monster. You leave, I can't say they'll change that, and you may find yourself in some trouble I can't get you out of because I'm too damn far away. Is that a chance you want to take?"

Well, when you put it like that... "Of course not. But this is your family. Aren't you worried they're going to hurt you guys trying to get to me?"

He looked at me and smiled, saying, "They won't, but if they did, I'd handle it. If you're on my bike or with a brother of this MC, you don't worry. Ever. That's not what this life is about. You've been fighting life on your own for a long time. It's time to let someone else carry that burden for a little bit, yeah?"

What could I say?

I smiled at him, but I was sure he caught the sheen of tears coating my eyes. He looked at me, studying my face for the longest moment before he stood up and gave Zeus a pat on the head. "You two sure do make one hell of a team; I'll give you that." He stopped in front of me and lifted a hand to cup my cheek using his thumb to trace my cheekbone. "Lie down and get some rest, Sweetness. I gotta talk to my brothers and fill them in. Your duffle is by the door if there's anything in there that you need before morning. Do I need to lock you in again to make sure you stay put or are we on the same page now?"

I shook my head and laughed. "Same page, Jinx. Same page."

"Good." He walked over to the boots he'd stepped out of earlier and slid his feet back in, bending at the waist he adjusted his pant leg and then turned to leave.

After he walked out of the room, I pulled the covers back and snuggled up to my already snoring dog. Beds were a rarity for the two of us, so we always snuggled and slept like rocks when we had the chance to use one.

I was trying desperately not to overanalyze my feelings.

CHAPTER TEN

Roxanne

When I woke up, I was curled around Zeus, lying on my side, facing the wall, and there was a body behind me. That caught me off guard. I'd fallen asleep alone in the bed except for the dog. *Who the hell is this?*

If I had to pick any of the brothers, it'd be Jinx, of course, but this attraction I was feeling in his presence was ridiculous. My stomach fluttering when he walked into the room, the rush of heat I felt when I caught scent of his cologne, the way I couldn't tear my eyes from him and made it awkward because everyone who saw me knew that I was panting after the biker god who had rescued me from the side of the road, both literally and figuratively.

I angled my eyes down without moving my head to try and see if I could identify the arms. I mean, the guys were almost all tatted up, except Scratch who definitely wouldn't be in my bed, so that should be easy, right? But my line of sight was hindered by my own boobs. If I weren't afraid to move right now, this would be the perfect facepalm moment.

I could at least take comfort in my dog thinking whoever was behind me was safe because he would have warned me otherwise. So that meant it was Jinx, right? It turned out I didn't have to wait long to find out because the arms stiffened, and a nose landed in my neck, inhaling deeply, then the body behind me loosened its grip on me and stretched with a groan.

A raspy, very familiar, could-be-etched-in-my-DNA-at-this-point, voice said roughly, "Mornin', Sweetness."

I relaxed back against his body. I hadn't even been aware that I was holding myself so tight, but I was happy it was Jinx. Let me correct that. Any girl would be happy it was Jinx; I was ecstatic it was him, and I couldn't stop the smile that took over my face.

"Jinx?"

He curled around me again and asked lazily, "Mmhmm?"

"Uh, how did we come to be in the same bed? Didn't you leave last night?"

"Had Scratch put you in my room. Can't keep you safe if you're in someone else's."

Oh. Well, I couldn't argue with that, so I voiced my thought, "Oh."

He started shaking behind me with laughter. "You always this cute and cuddly in the morning?"

My cheeks flamed up, and I couldn't say anything. No one had ever called me cute or cuddly. That made me sound like a teddy bear, or like my dog.

He inhaled at my neck again and ran his nose across it as he did so, igniting my body and lifting chill bumps from scalp to toe. Then he ruined it by giving me one more squeeze and releasing me to climb out of bed. "Come on, baby. Time to get up and get ready so we can hit the road."

Zeus lifted his head and swiped his tongue across my

cheek, his greeting to let me know it was time to get moving because his bladder would be waking up soon. "Jinx, I've gotta take Zeus out. He needs to take care of business."

"Right, I'll take the dog out, and you go get ready. Soap, shampoo, and anything else you need should be in the cabinet. I'll be back in a bit, and we'll grab a bite to eat before we hit the shop. C'mon, Zeus, let's take you out to piss while your mama gets dressed."

My dog, the one who didn't go to anyone except me, who obeyed my commands before the orders had been spoken, most of the time, jumped out of my arms and leapt over me to land on the floor beside Jinx, where he shook out his fur and then sat at the man's feet, staring up at him, his tongue hanging out, waiting to see what they were going to do next.

I lay in bed until they both walked out of the room. Jinx had Zeus on a leash just as a precaution since there was currently a bounty out on his head and we needed to make sure he was safe and contained at all times. After the door shut behind them, I climbed out of bed and grabbed my duffle on the way to the bathroom to get showered and ready to face this new day. I hadn't even been on this island for a week, yet suddenly everything was different about my life.

I had just—unknowingly, sure, but still had—spent the night in a man's arms. Even at the happy lovey-dovey stage of our relationship, I'd never been held like that by my ex.

My dog, who distrusted most people, had happily gone off for a walk, leaving me alone, which was something that'd never happened before.

I shrugged to myself. I mean, what else could I do? It was time to take a shower and get ready for work. I would have all day to mull over this situation while I sat at my desk.

CHAPTER ELEVEN

Roxanne

Wide Load was the person assigned to Zeus duty today, which seemed to suit them both. Zeus climbed up onto one of the couches and did a quick three circles before plopping down with a sigh and dropping his big head onto the big man's lap.

I hadn't considered the fact that I would be riding on a motorcycle for the first time in my life this morning, and for all my bravado, I was freaking out. I didn't know the policies and procedures to keep myself safely on the bike and off the ground, and I wasn't sure that Jinx was right when he grabbed my hands to pull them around his waist and said, "Just lean with it, Sweetness. It's instinct. We won't fall over."

I felt the vibrations through my core from the loud and fierce roar of the bike coming to life, and adorned with the helmet he'd put on my head, I dropped my forehead to the back of his cut and closed my eyes, praying while we started off.

I was sweating, cussing, and on my way to a panic attack when I realized that the wind was blowing and he was right. My body seemed to know what it needed to do, or it was following his, but either way, it was okay.

I lifted my head and watched as we roared down the street toward the shop and the rest of the downtown area, which I was learning was away from the touristy part of the island. I was enjoying this. It was freedom in a way that I'd never felt before. I felt like I could fly in those moments. Had we been on the open road with no one in sight, I would have thrown my arms out to embrace the wind's wild caress, but instead, I held on and laughed in sheer delight.

I was still smiling huge when we pulled into the parking lot at Mama's, and Jinx killed the bike. "Let's grab a bite to eat, Sweetness."

I would've followed him into the ocean fully clothed in the dead of winter at that moment, so pure was my bliss. I climbed off the bike and pulled the helmet off my head, handing it to Jinx, then bent at the waist and flipped my hair back up to try and get some of the creases and chaos out of it. He watched me silently, and when I stood upright again, I saw that he had dropped my helmet onto the bike. He reached out for my hand, and I took his and let him herd me into the restaurant.

I looked around when I walked in but didn't recognize any of the patrons and didn't see Maisie, the waitress who had offered to read my palm the other day. That was something I had never had done before, and I couldn't help but be curious to see if there was something she could discern from it, or if it was all the BS I had always believed.

Instead of eating outside this time, Jinx led me to a booth at the back of the restaurant and sat across from me. "So, are you a coffee drinker? Something else?"

"Coke. Regular, old fashioned, straight from the source,

American red Coca-Cola is my vice."

He quirked a lip and nodded when an older lady walked over to us, smiling, and asked, "Hey darlin', What do you kids want to drink this morning?"

Jinx answered for the both of us and then introduced her. "I want coffee, the stronger, the better, and she wants a regular Coke. Birdie, this is Roxanne; Roxanne, this is Birdie, Wide Load's old lady and mom to the fucktard, Scratch."

"Ahhhh." I smiled at her broadly and happily because Scratch was cool, and her old man was dog sitting for me today. "Well, I dig your son. He's cool. And your old man—"

She picked up on my hesitancy to say old man and explained. And relief washed over me because honestly, it felt almost like I was speaking a foreign language. "He's my hubby, darlin'. Biker Slang. You'll get used to it eventually if you plan to stick around."

Jinx had been lazily perusing the menu, but when she said that, he jerked his head up and said, "She's staying." He went right back to the menu after declaring that.

Birdie seemed to take his word for it and said, "I dropped in last night to make sure I didn't need to do a supply run and saw the sperm receptacles, but I didn't see you. Gypsy, right?"

"That's what they have all decided they should call me. Well, except for him." I pointed at the man across from me. "Evidently for him, I'm Sweetness."

Birdie smiled at me softly and said, "You'll come to appreciate it, darlin'. Givin' you a road name means they staked a claim on you. We get our legal names from some person who has no clue what we're gonna be like when we're full-grown, and they're giving us a name that reflects their hopes and dreams. We get our road names from people who have decided they like who we are as people, and we mean something to them. You spent a lot of time on the road, and you have those gorgeous, slanted dark eyes. You look just like a gypsy to me. Anyways, I didn't see you, and it's not kosher to talk club biz with an outsider, so I'll just say that I have an inkling that you have some trouble, and I hope you know if Jinx and my boy ain't around and you need something, all you gotta do is give me or that husband of mine a shout, and we got you. Now, let me go get y'all's drinks while you check out the menu and see what you want to eat for breakfast."

She ambled away, and I could feel my eyes tearing up. I didn't understand this tightness in my chest. The way it felt like I needed to cry and smile at the same time. I focused on the light on the ceiling above us to try and regain some composure, but I could feel it crumbling, that grip I had on my self-control. For the life of me, I couldn't make sense of what was going on here. I had been on my own my whole life, and I didn't need anyone. I knew that. But these people, these rough and tumble people who at first glance appeared to be of the criminal variety, were accepting me into the fold and giving me something I never knew I was missing. A place to belong.

I didn't know what my plans were after this. I didn't know where the next part of my journey would lead, but I did know that if it weren't on this island and as a part of the family that these people had built, I would always remember them, and I would always miss them.

A tear slipped over the rim, and I tried to catch it and slowly breathe in so it wouldn't be obvious I was breaking apart, but I should have known better. Before I could catch it,

Jinx had lifted a hand across the table and caught my tear on his pointer finger.

"What's all this, Sweetness?"

I breathed in deeply, letting my lungs expand fully, and breathed out before answering him. "Honestly? I don't know what to do with all of this. I told you I grew up in the system. I bounced from foster home to foster home, and the only real honest to God bond I have ever made before crossing onto this island and meeting you was with my dog. I've never been the type to make connections. I'm not a gypsy. I'm a nowhere girl."

He searched my face in that way of his, letting me know he was looking to see if I had given him all of it. I had, and he seemed to realize that because his face softened, and he said, "Sweetness, we're the Mischief Makers, a rowdy band of misfits who claimed a jester as our emblem. We praise Jesus at the altar of bikes, booze, and broads. We've, every brother among us, seen battle, and anyone we claim, no matter how we claim them, we do because there is something about you that fits with us. Maybe you weren't a nowhere girl. Maybe you just hadn't found your place."

That seared through me.

Have I found my place here with these people?

I couldn't say for sure because I'd never had a place and because I didn't know what the future held for me, but I did know that I felt like I could belong here; that I fit in for the first time in my life. And as I picked up the menu to decide what it was that I wanted to eat for breakfast, I felt happy.

CHAPTER TWELVE

Roxanne

I was sitting behind the counter talking to Pops when I heard the bell over the door ring and looked up to greet the newcomer.

"Hey! What can we do for you?" I asked, smile at the ready.

The shaggy-headed man who walked through the door did a double-take when he saw me and then shut the door behind him and kept walking toward me. "Well, you can do a lot for me, pretty girl. Where have you been all my life?"

That was one reaction I'd not gotten from anyone who had stepped foot through the door, and I was stunned silent. Pops looked up and boomed out a laugh before yelling, "Well, sonuvabitch, look what the cat dragged in!"

The man making his way toward us grinned huge and said, "Codgy old coot. When did we get the new talent in here?"

He didn't stop when he got to the counter and walked around it straight up to Pops. He slapped his arm and pulled him in for a hug before the older man could answer him and instead spoke again, "Darlin', what are you doing tonight? Or say, for the rest of your life?"

The door opening to the garage saved me from responding

when Jinx walked in—thank God—and the stranger pulled away from Pops and grinned broadly at Jinx, who walked right up to me and slung an arm over my shoulder.

It was an odd move considering the most we'd touched aside from me throwing myself at him on the side of the road when we'd met was sleeping in the same bed last night and him somehow ending up with his arms around me. I felt his arm like a two-ton weight on me, but I was desperately trying to play it cool, even as it burned against my skin. If I wasn't careful, my heart was about to pound out of my chest.

The still unknown, to me anyway, newcomer took us in and nodded. "Good for you, brother. Bad for me because I see her playing a starring role in some of my dreams, but good for you."

"Yeah. Bad for you because I will break your fucking neck if you even think about dreaming about her. Real bad for you."

"Not even one?" the other man joked.

"Brother, I even think you've disobeyed, and I'll make Dad's worst walloping look seem like a gentle hug." There was a smile in his voice that made me think the whole thing had been some big joke between the brothers.

"Right, well, are you gonna say hi to your only living blood brother, or are you going to keep pissing on your girl's leg?"

Oh. I could see that now. There were a lot of similarities between Jinx and whatever his brother's name was.

Jinx dropped his arm and walked toward his brother, who met him halfway, and they hugged tight. It took several moments before they let go, and I could feel it, the love and affection swelling in the room. These two loved each other.

When they pulled back, I had to put a hand to my chest
to keep my heart from bursting right out of it. I could feel
the look they were sharing. It was unlike anything I had ever
experienced before, and I realized that this was what reuniting
siblings who loved and missed each other did. I had none, so I
had never experienced it.

I was so caught up in my feelings that I didn't even notice
they were now talking and laughing. Finally, it occurred to me
that they were talking to me, and I tuned in. "I'm sorry. What?"

The brothers looked at each other and snickered.

"Sweetness, I was introducing you to my brother.
Roxanne, Nomad. Nomad, Roxanne. The boys call her Gypsy
and"—I got a pointed look here—"no, Nomad isn't his real
name. It's Ging—"

Nomad—whatever the heck his real name was—lifted
a hand and smacked his brother on the back of the head,
laughing and saying, "That ain't my fucking name, and you
know it, asshole."

Jinx retaliated by elbowing him in the gut, and Pops
groaned and yelled, "Alright, you little fuckers, cut that shit
out!"

That got them to stop, and they seemed to realize where
they were and with whom because they both dropped their
eyes and started adjusting their clothes. That was when I
started laughing, Pops rasped out a laugh, too.

Finally, Nomad looked at Jinx and asked, "Trouble?"

Jinx responded with a single word. "Heaps."

Pops and I weren't laughing any longer.

Jinx spoke again, saying, "How long are you in for?"

Nomad responded, "If you need me? I turn and burn, drop

this load, and put in some family time. You don't; I'm back out tonight and out of Texas tomorrow. So, you tell me."

Jinx nodded and said, "I'll fill you in, and you can head out. Shit's not getting too hot yet, so we don't need reinforcements."

"Right. And the phone call I heard about from Scratch? You gonna fill me in on that one, too?"

Three sets of eyes turned to me, and Jinx said something I would be hearing a lot in the future. "Club business."

Nomad nodded and said, "10-4."

Jinx smiled at me and said to the room at large, "The old man ain't getting a damn thing done since Roxanne sashayed her sweet ass in here the first time. We're standing here, and no one has anything on the books for over an hour, and you're in town for just a little bit. Let's go to Mama's and catch up, and we can talk business later before you leave."

I immediately felt like an intruder, so I put my hands up and said, "Hey, you guys go catch up. I'm fine here and can hold down the fort. I'll only be a third," I looked to Pops and corrected, "err-fourth wheel."

Jinx shook his head, but he had lost the easy expression on his face as he said, "Sweetness, I'm pretty sure we got somewhere at breakfast. I think you see that there's something between us and that your 'I don't belong' shit doesn't fly here. So, shut up and grab whatever you need to eat. Nome, you bobtail?"

Bobtail?

"Yup, but if Pops is riding in my rig, he needs a damn seatbelt. I'm not carrying his ass to the hospital because he can't sit still."

Pops yelled at him, "Look here, fucker! I was slinging gears long before you were even a twinkle in your daddy's eye, and I could outdrive you any day of the week. Gypsy gets the seat because fuck only knows what you get up to in that sleeper, and she might catch something Ajax can't take off."

"Y'aren't worried about catching something, old man?" Nomad grinned evilly.

"Son, that shit runs from me. I'm Chuck Norris to an STD."

At that, we all lost it and didn't stop laughing as we walked out to his truck and until I got a shock.

"Holy shit, dude! You drive a big truck?" I couldn't contain my excitement, and I didn't even care. I had never been this close to one in person, and I couldn't wait to climb in. I lightly bounced on my tippy-toes, overjoyed that I was going to get to see inside one of these.

Nomad smiled cockily. "Yes, ma'am, I do. She's a beaut, isn't she? I got her from our old man, and Jinx and I completely rebuilt her."

This got me to look at Jinx. "For real?" I was the kid in the candy store. I couldn't contain my excitement, and the man who could tame Pitbulls and diagnose Sally on the side of the road and rub his nose across my neck in a way that lifted chill bumps across my whole body, he just got even better. He could do something like this with his own hands.

I noticed when I looked back at the truck that the MC logo was displayed huge and proudly on the back of the cab. The lettering and the jester skull took up all the space, but still in the top left corner, I saw that this differed from the guys' patch because in screaming red it said, "Stainless Steel", and in the bottom right corner in the same scrolling font and screaming color it declared, "Sex Appeal".

I could have fainted.

CHAPTER THIRTEEN

Roxanne

The ride over had been hilarious.

Scratch saw that we were heading out and decided to come along for a ride, so he and Pops hopped into the bed at the back of the cab and sat crisscross applesauce, looking like two over-grown, extremely hairy, and dingy outlaws in their cuts.

I climbed in before Jinx, and he used a hand to brace me, incidentally touching my upper thigh and lower butt cheek while boosting me up. His grip on my bare leg caused another flare of those goosebumps, and I hurriedly pulled myself up and slid over the seat before he could see them.

With the two miscreants sitting on the only other available seat, I hesitated there awkwardly, really wishing that I had just stayed inside the office, but as soon as Jinx dropped into the seat and slammed the passenger door shut, he grabbed my hand and pulled me into his lap sideways.

I sat awkwardly across his lap as Nomad put the already idling truck into gear and pulled out of the parking lot. On the short drive over to Mama's, three different people honked and waved, and any bike that drove past, a hand was thrown up in greeting. And there I sat, right across Jinx's lap.

When we pulled into the parking lot, and the truck stopped rolling—I had no clue where park was on the insane gearshift—Jinx tapped my hip, and I took the hint and stood up to let him up.

He opened the door and swung out to climb down the cab, and instead of hitting the last step, he just let go and jumped down and then looked up at me, grinning. "Your turn, Sweetness."

Shaking my head at his silliness, I held on to the oh-shit handle, put my foot in the footrest right under the passenger door, and grabbed hold of one of the bars to swing down to the steps that led to the ground. I scurried my way down, and when I hit bottom, I looked up to see Pops laughing at me.

Whatever.

When we walked in, Jinx held the door open for me, and I walked in first, followed by the rest of the guys, who blocked me protectively.

Maisie was behind the counter, and when she saw me, smiled broadly and started to greet me, but when the rest of our crew finished filing in, and she saw Nomad, she yelled, "Holy shit! The prodigal returns!"

Scratch was the only brother who didn't seem to find that amusing. Instead, it seemed to piss him off, and he made a concentrated effort not to make eye contact with Maisie. Nomad greeted her. "Crazy Maisie. Get over here and give us a hug, girl. Last time I came through, you were off at some hippie convention or something, weren't you?"

She laughed and said, "Fuck off, Daniel. It was South by South West, and I was in Austin. You could have swung through there to say hi."

"Crazy Maisie, you can't swing through Austin. That place is a zoo and in a rig? No way in hell."

Pops gestured at Jinx and then walked away to the restrooms.

"Lies," she brushed him off and walked around the bar to us. "Where's that big, handsome guy you brought to see me the other day, Roxanne?"

I laughed. "Pops? Or do you mean Zeus? He's—"

Jinx cut me off, firmly saying, "He's not around today, and that's all that needs to be said right now."

I left it alone because she seemed to understand that this fell under "club business" and as such wasn't to be discussed.

She instead stepped around us and led us outside, where Jinx and I had sat the other day, and asked, "Beer for you, boys? What about you, Rox?"

I smiled and said, "Coke, please?"

She nodded and looked up as Nomad spoke, "Not for me, Maiz. I'll have what she's having. I'm headed back out tonight."

Maisie playfully groaned and rolled her eyes, then turned and walked back inside to get our drinks.

Jinx's phone rang, and he stood to take it from his pocket and said, "Fuck. I gotta take this. Bro, you stay with Roxanne, yeah?" He was looking his brother dead in the eyes and relaying something I couldn't read. Whatever it was, the message was received because Nomad nodded and gave me a friendly smile.

"Little sister and I have tons to catch up on."

Jinx got up, and Scratch followed him back into the restaurant when Nomad said, "So, how did you end up mixed up with this bunch? You look like a sweet girl, but we aren't exactly boy scouts, and my big bro is definitely not one."

"I may look like a sweet girl, but everything isn't always as it seems. I grew up rough, and I've spent the last year or so just drifting, trying to figure out where I belong."

"And do you belong here?"

I thought about that before I answered, "I think I could. I don't know if I do or not yet, though."

"My brother cares about you. How long have you known each other?"

I laughed. Oh boy. "Less than a week."

That surprised a laugh out of him. "Well, I guess things happen for a reason, right?"

"Oh Lord, have you been hanging out with Maisie?"

He laughed again and told me with a wink, "Not as much as I did when we were in high school hanging out beneath the bleachers, not that Scratch likes to think about that. He's been chasing and avoiding her for as long as his dick's been getting hard."

CHAPTER FOURTEEN

Jinx

I stormed back out the door to snatch Roxanne out of her seat and drag her back inside. This motherfucker was already talking again, but I could hear his earlier words over and over again. The cold, slimy threat behind them. He'd only spoken the words once, but I had replayed them for the five hundredth time.

"Your girl looks hot as shit sitting there playing with her hair, talking to your brother. I wonder what she's thinking? I could read their lips for you if you'd like? Try to let you know if you have anything to worry about."

Your girl looks hot as shit.

"Motherfucker." My blood ran cold. He had eyes on us, and I needed to get her inside pronto.

She was laughing at something my brother said, but all I could think was that it would be easy for someone to put a bullet through her head right in front of me. It twisted me up in ways I wasn't prepared to consider yet.

Nome read my face and jumped up, ready to defend. I grabbed Roxanne's arm and dragged her up from the table. I didn't have time to sugarcoat things for her. I had to get her to safety and explain after. Thankfully, she came with me easily and didn't cause a scene. My intentions of getting her to safety seemed to get across.

Back inside the restaurant, I drug her to the back and deposited her in a booth, where I blocked her physically with my body. Motherfuckers would have to go through me and my brothers to get her. That was when I responded. "Man, if you force my hand, we will retaliate. She's mine. You need to back the fuck off. This will be the last bridge you burn in Texas."

"Do you think El Jefe is concerned with your merry band of men? This isn't a little street gang anymore, friend. Our metamorphosis is much grander than that. We aren't just associated with the cartel; we *are* them. So, if you and your brothers want to stay on MY island, a few things are going to change. Your bar and strip club? We want in. And your patrolling stops today. I find your boys off Double M property, and they will be shot on sight. No more club colors or any of that other bullshit. The days of playing dress-up are behind you."

Every word he spoke reinforced my anger. I was drooling, desperate for a release, and I had to play this fucker's game, at least for now.

"And the girl?"

"Fuck her sweet, my friend, and do it often because the minute we find her solo? She's ours, and we won't fuck her nice. The fucking dog will be shot when we find him, but I want to play with your girl."

The line went dead in my ear, and it was all I could do not to throw the fucking phone and tear apart everything in my line of vision. I breathed through it though and was able to keep my cool because I could tell from my girl's face that she was freaked way the hell out. Looking up, I realized that not only was Pops there and at attention, but my best friend and my brother, as well as several of the patrons and employees of the restaurant, were watching me and waiting to see if I'd lock it down, or if I'd lose control. Looking back at Roxanne, I breathed through it and thought quickly.

I was limited on my options, and the very last thing I wanted was for it to get back to them that I was losing my shit, or calling my brothers in. No. Fuck 'em.

We were going to sit, inside this time, and eat our meal, and then I would have to stay on top of Roxanne the rest of the day.

Tonight, every man wearing a cut, and every man who wanted or had the jester on his back would be sitting down because things had just hit a boiling point. It was official.

We were going to war *again*. Only this time it was for our club instead of our country.

CHAPTER FIFTEEN

Roxanne

There was a tension that felt stifling and suffocating. At least two brothers stayed on me for the rest of my shift, and at the end of the day, Nomad was still there.

Jinx had called for church tonight, and every brother and prospect was expected to be there.

I wasn't sure what was going on, but something was in the air, and it was terrifying. There was a seriousness to the boys that I hadn't seen before — a watchfulness and a wariness that they usually hid under the good old boy exterior.

Jinx had handed me a gun when we walked back into the office after lunch and given me strict orders to shoot if I needed to defend myself.

It hit me when I was sitting with Pops and Nomad talking about some of the places I had seen since they'd both spent significant amounts of time on the road and knew some of my favorite places, that I could leave. I could go get my dog, load up, get the hell off this island, and leave all of this behind.

I had nothing holding me here.

And yet, I knew that I wouldn't. Because that thought was a lie. These guys had gotten to me in a way that no one else ever had before, and I couldn't imagine leaving them. In the short time that I'd been with them, they'd sucked me in and made me part of their family.

That feeling was tripled when Birdie and Maisie showed up at the compound to sit with me while the boys were in church.

Zeus sat at my feet; even he seemed to pick up on the emotions and was in protection mode as I sipped on a Jack and Coke that Birdie had given me and told me to drink. "Those boys are going to be in there for a while. You drink this slowly, so you can keep your wits about you."

I appreciated the gesture and sipped the drink to calm myself.

Maisie had brought a stack of cards with her, and she was idly shuffling them back and forth. The three of us in a holding pattern, waiting to see what would come of this meeting.

We waited another twenty minutes and tried to occupy the time with chitchat, but our minds were otherwise occupied, so it wasn't until Birdie said, "Alright, Maisie. Hit me with a reading," that we found something to engross ourselves in.

Maisie flipped out a card and said, "Birdie, The Hanged Man. You're suspended and waiting for something."

Birdie snorted out a laugh and said, "Aren't we all?"

I nodded because we totally were.

Maisie turned to me and said, "Alright, your turn, sister!"

Flipping out a card, she laid it face up, and my blood went cold. "Death."

She looked up at me with a smile on her face, and all I could think was, *What the hell is funny about me dying?* But she seemed to pick up on my distress and explained, "Babe, it's not bad. Death doesn't mean death as in you die. Death means death as in the death of your old life and birth of your new one."

I considered that for a moment and then let out a sigh. Well, that was certainly happening as well.

Maisie picked the Death card up, slid it back into the deck, and said, "Now, my turn." And after considering it for a long moment, she drew a card from the pack and set it down, face up. And then she let out a startled laugh. "Fucking hell."

It was The Lovers.

CHAPTER SIXTEEN

Jinx

"You all realize what this means, right?"

As one, all my brothers nodded. They did, and it was huge.

Scratch spoke up first. "I'll start reaching out to our support clubs and getting people to come here. If this becomes a turf war, we're going to need all the help we can get to prevent this from dragging in citizens. The only problem I see is that if a bunch of bikes start riding onto the island, we're going to ignite this before we're ready."

At this, Nome lifted a hand and cut in. "Things have escalated to the point that I feel like it may be time to come home, at least stick close. So, what if we have a rallying point, and I load bikes up in my trailer and carry them onto the island? We can hide them at the compound and have the brothers fly in or drive in together, maybe even have a prospect or old lady bring them over by the carload. Just make sure we don't fly colors and draw attention to ourselves. This asshole is going to think he has the upper hand, but if we can coordinate this just right, we can cut them off at the knees and stop this war before it has a chance to escalate."

I considered this. It would be more time consuming than

just having a bunch of bikers ride onto our island, but many a battle was won with stealth.

"I like it. I called Q Ball before we came in for a sit-down and let him know. He's cutting his mountain vacation short and headed back today. We need to be prepared, brothers. This could get ugly quick. If you have any objections, speak now."

Nome spoke again, saying, "Not for nothing, but don't you think it would be safer to send the new piece away?"

This surprised me and pissed me off. "Brother, I believe I already made it clear that she stays. She's mine, and she's family now. I don't think this needs to be covered again."

He put his hands up in surrender and said, "Just making sure, bro. But seriously? What if I loaded her and the dog up and took them on the road while we start transporting reinforcements to the island? She would be safe, which would allow you to focus on what's going on here."

I lifted an eyebrow. I could see that he was genuinely trying to work the logistics of it all out and that made me happy because eventually, I wanted him to be my VP, but there was no way in hell I was letting her out of my sight, and he had to know that. So, I said, "Right. If anyone else has anything they need to bring to the table, now is the time. When we leave this room, we start putting our plans into motion, and there is no going back from that."

I looked around the table. I locked eyes with each of my brothers, with the men who were my brothers now but had also been my father's brothers. I looked at the prospects who were doing their time so they could have that same title. I didn't know what this was going to bring, but I did know that every single one of them was behind me one hundred and ten percent, and there was no turning back now that we had our plan laid out.

I banged the gavel onto the hand-carved table and said, "Alright, then, boys. Let's get this show on the road. We're pulling a Helen of fucking Troy, so let's hope this Trojan Horse does its job."

My brothers stood from the table and slowly made their way out of the room. I sat at the table thinking about this. It was a complex game we were playing, and if any of the moving pieces fell through, it could be game over. When I looked up, Pops, Scratch, and Nome were still sitting there watching me.

Pops broke the silence. "Shit's gonna get bad, son."

I nodded. What else could I say? We were going up against the big bads and could only hope and pray that we came out unscathed and without suffering too great a loss.

"This has been a long time coming. I want you to know that we're all in. This ain't just about territory for me. That's a good girl out there. One who has been kicked to shit and back and still smiles and laughs with a guy like me. She's your future. That makes her our future, too, and that means we take care of her."

I nodded. Generally, if I needed a fix, I'd hit up one of the bitches who roamed around here and didn't belong to anyone else, but since I'd pulled over to help her on the side of the road, Roxanne'd been the only one I've had any interest in. She wasn't the initial conflict between our two sides, but she had been the flame that struck tinder.

I leaned back and pulled a smoke out of my pocket, and drawing in and exhaling, I said, "Well, brothers. Let's get this party started."

CHAPTER SEVENTEEN

Roxanne

Most of the guys that came out of the room and headed our way were jovial and kidding around. It didn't seem like there was any major trouble going on, and yet I watched as the last one out of the room shut the door, leaving Pops, Jinx, Scratch, and Nomad inside.

Maisie watched the door carefully, for Nomad or Scratch, I wasn't sure. I knew that Birdie was watching because she was waiting for Scratch now that Wide Load had stepped up to the bar for a beer. I didn't understand what any of this was about, and I was being patient, but there was a limit to how far I was going to go down this path before I understood where the hell I was going.

The three of us didn't even pretend to make conversation as we waited, watching the door. And all three of us let out a simultaneous sigh when the men walked out of the room and headed in our direction.

I broke away from the girls to meet Jinx halfway, Zeus getting up to trail behind me, and asked, "Can we talk?"

He took in my face, and whatever he saw there made him nod and turn on a heel, leading the way to the door that led to the rooms. He walked to his door and opened it, letting me and then Zeus walk in before he trailed in behind us and shut the door.

"What's on your mind, Sweetness?"

"I've told you the situation I left behind."

He waited a moment and then agreed, "Yeah."

"What am I getting into here?"

"I'm assuming that my bed isn't the answer you're looking for, so I'm gonna say we've been in a stalemate with the Bangers for a while now. They brought drugs—and I'm not talking pills and pot; I'm talking meth and worse—onto the island, and we've been pushing them back while maintaining a tentative peace. But things have been heating up for months now, and threatening you, which is what they did today on the phone, crossed a line. You and your dog both have targets on you, but we'll keep you safe."

"Why?" I asked in curiosity. Why would these guys fight to keep me safe, though? They were a family, and I was an outsider.

I could see from the expression on Jinx's face that the question didn't make sense to him. As in a does-not-compute way. He was puzzled. It puzzled me that he was puzzled, though, so I asked again, "Why are you guys willing to fight to keep me safe? I don't know any of you. I've been here only days, and you have suddenly decided that I'm yours to protect. I don't understand why. I could pack up, put Zeus in the car, be across the bridge by midnight and halfway across the state by daybreak. There's no way to track me, no reason to track me if I'm not here, and you guys can go back to normal. I got this stupid death card while Birdie is hanging, and Maisie is falling in love or something, and I just… How the hell did all of this happen?"

I was panicking. It was washing over me, wave by wave, this sense of belonging, and I didn't know how to slow the emotions or feelings. I was caught in the undertow and couldn't get my head above water to scream for help.

Seeing this, Jinx sighed and locked the door before walking straight to me, kicking his shoes off on the way and pushing me onto the bed.

I sat down, and he sat on the floor facing me, pulling one of my Chucks to him and unknotting the string before sliding it off and chunking it at the wall. Once that was done, he gently set my leg down, grabbed the other, and repeated the process.

After releasing my other foot, he put both hands on my bare calves and asked confusingly, "Do you have any pajamas to put on, or do you want one of my tees?"

Uh, what?

"What are you talking about?"

He grinned and released my legs, standing up. "I'll get you a tee."

I just sat there like a moron. I spent more time trying to understand his next move than I ever had with anyone else. Was he this confusing as a person, or had I just been on my own for so long that I'd forgotten basic communication skills?

He walked to the dresser pressed against the wall and opened the top drawer, taking out a black tee, and threw it at me. I caught it and instinctively opened it to see what was on it.

It was the jester.

Flipping it out, I saw that it was long enough that I could

get away with wearing it as a nightshirt, so I ducked into the bathroom to change.

When I stepped back into the room, I felt like my legs were on fire. It had looked so much longer before my body was inhabiting it. Now I felt like the slightest move in the wrong direction was going to show Jinx my undies, and that wasn't a comfortable thought. I looked up to see that he was gone from the room and breathed out a sigh of relief before rushing to the bed to get under the covers. While he was gone, I patted the bed next to me, and when he finished his three spins, Zeus dropped to the bed with a sigh and was snoring within moments.

The light was still on, and I was debating getting up to turn it off when the door opened, and Jinx padded in barefooted, wearing a wife-beater and his jeans.

He smirked at me and turned the light off on his way to me. Once he reached the bed, he turned the lamp on and pulled the white ribbed tank over his head, saying, "Skootch over. You two are taking up the whole bed, and I need some room."

It had previously dawned on me that with Zeus taking up so much room in the bed where it met the wall that Jinx may be deterred from lying with me, but evidently, we were going three deep again, so with a sigh, I scooted over and pushed at Zeus. He looked up at me bleary-eyed and then stood up and jumped off the bed, walking to the corner and doing a quick three spins to lie down again. I shook my head. As if this couldn't get any more awkward.

Jinx laughed softly and lifted the corner of the blanket while I scooted, and he slid in behind me. I faced the wall because that felt safer, but after he switched off the light, he slid an arm under me and turned me around, so I was resting my head on his naked chest.

Then he said, and I could hear the smile in his voice, "Okay. Now, we talk."

CHAPTER EIGHTEEN

Roxanne

"Okay, first, did you really let Maisie do her woo-woo shit on you? And Birdie? She should know better. Maisie means well, but she's a little whacked. She's been getting "feelings" and reading auras or whatever the fuck since we were kids."

"Well, I mean, it seemed like harmless fun until it got a little too real. And Jinx, I don't think she thinks it's woo-woo. I think she believes it."

"She does believe it, Sweetness. Her mama made a living doing that kind of shit for the tourists until she couldn't anymore, and she taught Maisie to spout the same shit, thinking it would pave her way. Instead, she's slinging food and drinks at Mama's."

"Hey, it's not like that's a bad place or anything. I've worked my share of dives along the way, and Mama's is relatively nice compared to most. I don't know, maybe you're right, but I can't shake this feeling that she was dead right and that it has everything to do with this current situation."

"That's another thing. We talked about this already, but it bears discussing again. You aren't some charity case. You showed up essentially on my doorstep and immediately became one of the fold. You wonder how we figured out that you weren't staying at the motel? Pops was worried about you. Scratch was the first to hop on his bike and follow, to make sure you were safe. Hell, even Nome asked me today if I wanted to send you and Zeus with him while shit heated up. Because make no mistake, it's heating up. Tonight, we set a plan in motion that's going to change everything. We aren't aiming for peace with these fuckers anymore. They pushed, and it's time to push back. We don't take threats from anyone, regardless of who they are or what their affiliation with the club is. They just happened to come after you, and you're mine. You know it, I know it, and so will everybody else. The time for games is done."

It had to be asked. "I'm…" I hesitated for a brief moment and then finished on a breath, "yours?"

His hand that had been resting on my hip moved up and tugged at the end of my hair, tipping my head back so he could take my lips.

"Does it feel like you aren't? Because I can make my point a little firmer if I need to."

When he said that, butterflies danced through my body, and I warmed from head to toe. Without my say-so, my body seemed to melt into his, and when we kissed, really kissed for the first time? I was the one who initiated it.

He seemed content with soft kisses and sweet touches, but every time he touched me, the flames grew higher and higher, and I could take it no more. When I pulled away from him, he didn't fight me. He fell back against his pillow, dragging air into his lungs harshly, so he wasn't expecting it when I kicked a leg over him and landed with my lady bits right over his... excitement.

When contact was made, involuntarily, we both moaned, and I arched my back to rub against him at the same time, his hips bucked up to mine. The contact lit a powder keg, and in seconds, he had pulled his tee back over my head and ripped— yes, ripped—my panties off me. Before I could take it all in, he flew into action, flipping our positions, putting me on my back in the bed, completely naked and panting for him.

He shoved his boxers down, not even getting them off, and a moment later, he was inside me. I came as soon as he buried himself, and I was gasping for breath, unable to even think when he leaned down and swiped his tongue along my neck. I moaned deep in my throat, and it was all I could do not to scream. Somehow, someway, mere moments later, he was building another earth-shattering orgasm in me.

We fucked like crazy, made love like it was our wedding night, and then laughed ourselves stupid when, as we were coming down from the high of back-to-back orgasms, Zeus snored loudly, letting us know he hadn't even woken up. I knew the boys were going to give me hell in the morning, though.

I just knew it.

CHAPTER NINETEEN

Roxanne

The club was busy over the next couple of weeks. Pops had become one of my constant companions, and I loved him already.

Last night, we had sat in here and drunk beer while attempting to play Never Have I Ever.

Let me just say that a biker does not have many of those, so we switched to playing quarters instead, which waffled into a game of Bullshit. So, when he suggested Chihuahua races, I thought it was the most excellent idea ever. I was drunk, so everything sounded like a great idea. With the extra people filling up the building, Pops lined people up on either side to cut off the exit and took Zeus to the end. I was on the start side and crouched down to love on his idiot dogs, and when I looked up, I caught Pops pouring beer into a Solo cup and letting Zeus drink it. Those two had suddenly become bosom buddies because my dog was a beer slut. I grinned.

Patting the two mini mutts, I sat on the floor and watched as the bikers started to place bets on which dog would make it to Pops first.

Along the path to the old man, both dogs detoured to love on bikers; mostly, the bikers were trying to distract the dog they had bet against, and when one finally made it to Pops, several of the men groaned and handed over money, and the guys broke apart with laughter and good-natured ribbing.

Birdie or Rammer or someone else, never me or any of the club officers, would cross the bridge back to the mainland in an SUV with tinted windows and show up a few hours later with more men. As the compound became more and more packed with outsiders, I retreated to the safety of our room more frequently. With a compound full of bikers, things got rowdy and gross pretty quick.

I still went into the office, always with Jinx, in the mornings, and we left together in the evenings. He was in more and more meetings now with his brothers and the out-of-towners, but every night, he came to bed eventually, and when he did, he always found me in his tee sans panties—because he liked to rip them off me, and I was down to only a few pairs now. We made love, and he held me while we slept.

I was beginning to wonder if this was what real love felt like. The way I yearned for him when we were apart and then felt blissfully happy, even with the circumstances, when I caught sight of him. The way I could tell what his pipes sounded like when he rode away or came back with his brothers. The flurry of excitement I felt when he met my eyes or peeled my shirt off, or even just breathed in my general vicinity. Inexplicably, in all the chaos and scariness of the situation, I was caught up in my very own fairy tale of sorts; only my knight rode a hog instead of a steed and wore leather instead of armor.

Tonight was different, though, not with Jinx and me, but as a whole. There was something palpable in the air. A tingle of excitement and some sixth sense that warned me that things would be coming to a head, ready or not.

Nomad was late.

For the last few weeks, every few days, Nome would swing through with a trailer full of bikes and back it into the garage on the compound, and they would unload them. Turns out, being an old factory had an unexpected upside because the dock was already there.

The Mischief Makers were playing a game of intrigue and sneaking bikers over by car and their bikes by truck.

I was sitting at the bar when Jinx picked up his phone from beside me and barked, "Where the fuck have you been?"

Nomad. It has to be.

"Yeah," Jinx said. And then once more but in a much lighter tone of voice this time, "Yeah." And then he said, "Right. See you in a few, then." And disconnected.

Q Ball, the club VP, jerked his head in Jinx's direction, asking a silent question, and Jinx's equally silent answer was to tilt up the corner of his lips and shake his head. Whatever it was, it wasn't serious. Yet.

I leaned in closer to Jinx and asked, "Do I want to know?"

He laughed and said, "He picked up a bitch. He'll be here in an hour."

Bitch was the way, I'd learned, in which they described most females. There were other words they used, dependent on that female's status within the club, but for the most part, bitch was the go-to. I shrugged. I'd learned in my period of cohabitation with not only the Mischief Makers but also the other clubs that had trickled in, that these guys were whores. It was a significant part of the hesitation behind my asking Jinx what we were doing and how long it was going to last.

I let the thought go. It was the best thing for my well-being.

He watched me in that way of his, studying my face for reactions and trying to discern, I didn't know what, from my expression. I worked to keep it neutral, and he looked away without saying anything further.

Twenty minutes later, the door burst open, and Scratch stormed in, walked straight to Jinx, and said, "We got a problem. Need to talk, *now*."

That wave of unease came back tri-fold, and my palms went clammy. I wanted to ask 'What's wrong?' But couldn't. Not only could I not form the words, but it wasn't my place.

Jinx jerked his head to Q Ball and dropped a kiss to my forehead, stubbing out his cigarette, before standing from his chair and leading the other two to their office.

I looked around, but Birdie was gone, and Maisie wasn't here tonight. Pops was sitting on one of the couches, talking to some out-of-towners, meaning I was officially on my own.

I settled in with a sigh and stared at the wall while I worried.

CHAPTER TWENTY

Jinx

Scratch brought up the rear, and when he crossed into the room, he shut the door calmly and then picked up an empty beer bottle and threw it against the wall. The glass shattered and rained down on the floor, but he still didn't speak.

"Brother?" I asked. Something was going on here. I hadn't seen him like this since, well, ever, that I could remember. Scratch was the level-headed one. It's what made him so damn good at his job.

He threw a hand up in my direction and breathed deep before saying, "They got Maisie. I know we have a plan, and I know everything isn't in order yet, but man, they have *my* girl, and I want her back."

This hit me like a ton of bricks.

Not that he cared about her; I'd always known that and had repeatedly told him that his reasons for staying away were ridiculous, but because they had actually taken one of ours.

This wasn't like them grabbing a friend of the club. Maisie was family.

They had thrown down, and it was time to take it to them.

"Q, get the brothers. For now, just our club and just our

chapter. I want everyone here in ten minutes. Tonight's the night."

***

It took five for every brother on the island to be at the table.

"There's been a change in plans. Tonight, the Bangers crossed a line and took Maisie." This elicited mutters and curses from my brothers. "After Birdie and Pops get back tonight, we'll have just about everyone who's coming. Nomad will be here within the hour. I've just called him, and he's hammering down to get back home. Before we take this to everyone, though, we need a plan. We can't afford to charge in unprepared. If this isn't handled right, Maisie dies, and that does not happen on my watch."

There were nods from everyone around the table. I looked at Scratch. "You've been doing recon, brother. Tell us what to expect and what our best options are and keep your feelings out of it. You go in with emotions; someone is going to get killed. Think about this as a mission and Maisie as our target. We need to secure the target and get back with minimal blowback."

He nodded and asked me, "Is Alabama on board for this?"

Alabama was a friend in high places, in a way. A high-ranking pawn in the fight against the drug trade, my high school friend, had gone cop, and he was a man to be trusted if he was on board.

"He is, and his stance is the same. Minimal blowback. I give him a heads-up when we vacate, and the boys in blue ride in and clean shit up."

He nodded and mulled this over for a moment before he put his plan together and filled us in.

Every one of us was wearing a smile because these fuckers didn't even know that taking Maisie meant signing their lives away. We had them dead nuts.

CHAPTER TWENTY-ONE

Roxanne

I knew it when I saw his expression.

Something was going down, and it was big. Huge.

The brothers broke apart as they left the room used for church and made their way around the common area, starting to spread the word about whatever was going down.

Ice spread through my veins. I didn't know what their plan was; Jinx had kept me clear of that, and honestly, I didn't want to know as long as everyone made it home safe and sound. But I couldn't help but feel like this was it. Everything was finally coming to a head.

The brothers spread out and talked in groups of one or two to the other men.

Bigger groups of men standing around were starting to form, and some were making their way out of the building to get their bikes from where they were being stored.

At the roar of a Diesel engine, I knew that Nomad was there finally. Jinx looked up and made eye contact with me and jerked his head toward our room.

Following, I said nothing until we were shut inside, Zeus standing by the door, not even taking the reprieve to sleep as he usually would.

"How bad is it?" That was all I could think to ask.

He watched me, gauging my reaction and deciding on the fly how much or what to tell me. Finally, he sighed and said, "Honestly, Sweetness? About as bad as it gets. The Bangers grabbed Maisie tonight."

My sweet Maisie. My knees buckled, but I steadied myself as he reached out a hand to grab me. "Is she—" I couldn't voice it.

"No. Nothing like that. We're riding out tonight. It ends today, and we're getting her back. I need you to be strong and stay safe, though. I can't face going out there and fighting these bastards if I don't know you're safe and locked down here. Can you promise me that you'll stay? No matter what?"

I wanted to lash out. I wanted to tell him that there was no way in hell, but I couldn't. Maisie was my friend, but she may as well be his sister, and this was eating at him. The last thing he needed was for me to fall down on him now. So, I nodded. If what he needed was for me to be here holding down the fort, then that was what he was going to damn well get.

He smiled and brushed the hair from my cheek, pushing it behind my ear. "Brass balls. When that motherfucker was declaring open season on you? He told me my girl had brass balls. Through and through, you were made for the life, and you were made to be my old lady. Best fuckin' thing that ever happened to me, you and that car and that dog limping onto the island. You watch. Before this life is over, I'm gonna make all three of you shine. Fuckin' love you, Sweetness."

After dropping that bomb on me, he kissed me and led me back out of the room to the others.

A woman was walking across the room with Nomad. She had black hair, her left arm was sleeved out, and her bottom left lip was pierced. I looked at Jinx in askance, but he just shrugged. Whoever she was, she was important to him, judging by the way Nome claimed her with an arm over her shoulder when he saw us making our way back through the room. They started our way.

As she got closer, I realized that she had a bruise on her cheek and scratches on her hands and throat. I wasn't sure what that was about, but I knew a girl in trouble when I saw one. I stopped and stood on my toes to kiss Jinx's jaw before pulling away and introducing myself.

Sticking out a hand, I said, "Hey, I'm Roxanne."

She eyeballed me and then, after hesitating and looking up to Nomad, she put her hand out as well and said, "Hey, Roxanne, I'm Mitchey."

Nomad took over the introductions after that, saying, "Mitch, my brother, Jinx. He's the prez, and Roxanne is his old lady. Bro, my girl, Mitch."

Jinx gave her a nod in greeting and said, "Sweetness, why don't you get Mitchey a drink and introduce her to Zeus? Birdie'll be back in a bit, and we're going to be rolling out. I need you to hold everything down here. I'll have the prospects and a couple brothers on y'all for precaution, but I don't 'spect much of anything here."

I nodded. "And my gun?"

He grinned. "It's in our room, Rox."

I got a tap on the ass, and then the two men broke away from us and made their way to the others.

Left to our own devices, I decided that to start, I needed

my gun, and then we could use a drink.

It was going to be a long night.

CHAPTER TWENTY-TWO

Roxanne

I held it together and maintained my composure as long as I could. I did what I perceived as my duty and entertained the quiet woman Nome'd brought to us. Introducing her to my Zeus seemed to break the ice a little, but I could tell she was uncomfortable. We made idle chitchat, nothing in-depth because I had no clue what to say to her. She had just shown up while our guys were getting ready to head out on a do-or-die mission like modern-day vigilantes, and I, for one, was scared shitless.

I didn't fall apart until after all the men had rolled out. The thunder of dozens of bikes roaring in the night shook the walls. Then Birdie came over and sat next to me, right where she had not that long ago when Maisie had pulled cards from her tarot deck and proclaimed life-changing events for her and me.

There had been a foolishness to us that night, the way we were hanging out and having fun even though there was a war being declared. We were safe and sound in our fortress with knights who rode steel ponies and adorned themselves with tattoos as war paint. Secure in the knowledge that nothing outside could touch us. The boys had us, Birdie, me, and the other old ladies attached to the club under protection, but no one thought Maisie would need it. It had never crossed anyone's mind, and now we were all paying the piper because God only knew what they were doing to her while they had her.

Birdie sat next to me and held my hand. I drew strength from her. She wouldn't leave my side until the boys were back; after all, she had more to lose than anyone else. Her husband and her son were out there fighting side by side with Jinx and the rest.

My cell began to ring, and I didn't bother to see who was calling. There were so many people who had my number now that it could be anyone, and I couldn't afford to miss a single call.

I was shocked to hell and back when I heard the voice on the other end of the line, though.

"Roxy?" Fuck. Fuck.

"Norm?" I asked, even though I knew it was him.

"Baby, I just got sprung, and Mama says she hasn't seen or heard from you in months. I'm home now. It's time to come back."

No way in hell.

"Norm, I'm not coming back. I have a life. I'm not even in the state anymore. It's done."

"Roxy," he began again in his nasally placating voice, "c'mon, girl. It's time to get back home. Don't make me come after you."

Soon, really soon, he would start with the begging. He always did, which was when I used to cave just to shut him up. I had held my tongue and played the nice girl, but I was a motherfucking MC president's old lady, and my only real friend was in the bad guys' clutches, living through who even knew what. It was time to take off the gloves and give him the truth for once in his life.

"Norman, look. I do not have time for this, so I'm just going to tell you. I've moved on. I'm in a relationship with a man you do not want to mess with. A man who is out right now attacking bastards with what amounts to an army of bikers to get my friend back. I don't love you. I don't even like you. And I don't know if I ever did. I'm gone, and I'm never coming back. And one more thing? I took your fucking dog. Not only does he not fight, but every night when I crawl into bed with my biker, my dog is right there with us. He drinks beer with the boys, likes peanuts and pizza more than anything else, and he will never be scared or hurt again."

With that, I disconnected the call.

Maisie had called it all with a single tarot card. The ending of my old life and the beginning of my new one. I needed her to get back so I could tell her she was right.

CHAPTER TWENTY-THREE

Jinx

I t was a shit show if I had ever seen one.

We got the drop on them, but they knew something was going on. Hell, if they'd pushed Maisie, she would have been able to tell them that we were funneling reinforcements onto the island in droves. So, they knew what our plan was, at least in part, and the only ace we had was that they didn't know when. But regardless, they were prepared.

The only major plus we had was that they hadn't called us, so they didn't know that we knew. Scratch had gone to the diner to see Maisie, and when he found out that she hadn't come back from lunch, he had them pull surveillance footage and was able to identify one of the Bangers doing a snatch and grab as she walked around the side of the building.

So, when we roared up a good thirty bikes deep, they got a pretty good idea fast about what we were up to. Then everything had gone downhill.

They'd started firing on us as soon as we were in range, and currently, Scratch was around the building with Pops and some of the others trying to breach the back while we returned fire in the front. Nome had grabbed some odds and ends and was working to rig an explosive device, his specialty in the military, so that we could get some headway against these fuckers.

I knew for a fact that we'd taken a few of the fuckers out. I had no clue how many, but every bullet that was fired put one of our own at risk of getting hit by his own people, so I was cautious. This wasn't a Wild West shootout for my boys.

Nome gave the high sign, and we lay down cover fire while he ran for the door. He tossed it on the doorstep, then turned and ran for cover again.

When the device went off, the door blew back on its hinges, and debris rained down. As the smoke cleared, I was watching for any movement.

Nada.

Sweat was pouring down my face, but I couldn't take my eyes off the door long enough to swipe it away. I had to keep watch. The most minuscule movement could alert me to someone sneaking around to draw a sight on one of ours.

We watched for several moments, and then I threw up a hand and led the way to the entrance.

It was dead silent in there except for the creaking of the mortally damaged building. I felt my phone vibrating and dug it out one-handed, leaning against the wall next to the door. A quick glance showed me that it was Vincent.

I hit accept and said, "What?" Damned if I would let the fucker have the first word.

"Jinx, amigo, what the hell was that about, huh? You just drop in for a visit and tear my house apart?"

"Where is she, motherfucker? And where the hell are you?"

He laughed, and I felt a tingle of unease run down my spine when he said, "My boys had a good time with that one. I really wish I could be there to see Scratch when he finds his pretty psychic. I just called to let you know that on our way out, one of my boys got a little trigger happy, and your long-haired old man is lying in the back, bled out by now, I'm sure."

The line went dead, and my blood ran cold.

I ran through the questions in my mind as quickly as possible. *Is it a trap? Are they still in the house? Did they actually get out?*

Scratch yelled out from further in the house, "Found her! Get your asses in here!"

That sealed it for me; I turned and said, "Yo! You three on me, and the rest with Scratch. Fucker says they got Pops, and he's down. Go!"

We ran back out the front door and started to run around the side of the house when one of the boys shouted, "Jinx, they just went Splitsville on three ATVs! Bastards were out a window before we realized what was going on."

Fuck!

I didn't stop to talk. If they were gone, then they weren't a threat and not my problem at the moment.

My heart dropped when I got to the back of the house and saw the old bastard who was as close to a father as I had left, lying in a puddle of his own blood. One of the men behind me pulled out his phone and dialed emergency as I ran to him and knelt down to check for a pulse, and thank fuck, it was there.

"Come on, old man, get the hell up. We don't got time for this shit."

He groaned, and my heart skipped a beat with relief. "Shit.

Get over here and put some pressure on this bullet hole. I'm going to run in and check on Scratch and Maisie and see how bad things are in there!"

Scratch was holding Maisie on the floor in his arms while she was sobbing. I pushed my way to them, and when I saw Maisie, the ice water in my veins turned to lava.

Oh no, oh, hell no.

Her face was bloodied, and tears mixed with the crimson from fresh wounds. Her pretty pink hair had been hacked away in places, and she was only wearing one shoe. The shirt she'd worn that day was hanging loosely from her in shreds, and her pants were gone.

I didn't ask. Couldn't form the words. But in that moment, I knew that this wouldn't be over until I had put a bullet in Vincent's head and we eliminated every Banger on the island.

CHAPTER TWENTY-FOUR

Roxanne

Standing over his hospital bed, I didn't expect the first tear, but the second was equally astounding. As I dabbed a finger to my lid and felt the wet there, I realized I couldn't staunch the flow. Before I knew it, I was sobbing quietly, standing there looking down at his wrinkled and hairy face.

I would never understand how it had happened, and how it had happened so quickly, but these idiot men had somehow managed to make me fall in love with them all. Here I was, trying to silently cry so I wouldn't wake Pops up, and I was emotional because he was in the hospital with a gunshot wound.

When I looked up at him, his eyes were open, and he lifted a hand to pull the oxygen mask up from his face, so I could hear him. "Whatcha cryin' about, Gypsygirl?"

"You, you big, stupid moron. I don't have a dad, but I have you, and I figure that's about the same. I ca—" My words broke off, and I had to breathe in to calm myself. Then I wailed out, "I can't lose you."

His face softened, and he smiled, saying, "Oh, Roxanne. I'm all good, darlin'. Gonna be back on my barstool and my hog in just a few days. I'll drink a beer with Zeus, and we'll place bets on my Chihuahua races."

I laughed through the tears,. "It's a date," I said, smiling softly at him.

I left after a few more moments and went three rooms down the hall to see my friend. She wasn't talking to anyone right now, and I knew it was going to kill to see her lying in her hospital bed with that far-away look in her eyes, but I had to. She'd been there for me from the first time we'd met, and my friend needed me. If all I could do was sit in her room and give her silent company, then I was going to do it.

I walked over to her bed and saw that her eyes were red. She'd been crying again. My own eyes burned again when I saw that. I sniffled and then bent to her forehead to brush my cheek to her, saying, "Hey, Maisie. I just wanted to come sit with you for a little bit. I miss you being around everywhere I am. I need you to get better so you can read my cards—"

The animalistic wail that came from her chest scared me. Frantically, she started to jerk her head from side to side. I jumped up from my seat and started to panic. "Oh, God, no. What, Maisie? Do I need to get someone?"

She quickly shook her head faster and made an effort to get herself under control. She closed her eyes and inhaled deeply before whispering in the softest of voices, "No cards. No cards. No cards." Over and over again.

"Okay, hun. No cards. I hear you."

This calmed her enough that I dared to ask in the quietest voice I could muster, "Are you okay, Maisie?"

She shook her head back and for twice to let me know that no, she was not okay.

I tried again. "Can you talk about it?"

Again, she shook her head.

I drew in a breath and said, "Okay. Do you want me to leave?"

I met her eyes, and she shook her head twice more.

No.

CHAPTER TWENTY-FIVE

Jinx

It was Alabama who came through. He called me and told me that they had tracked down Vincent and the Bangers he had taken with him as protection. There were five in total, and they were holed up in an abandoned warehouse but couldn't get off the island because of police presence. His words were, "I'm going to wait five minutes, and then I'm walking out and getting in a cruiser. Don't be there when I get there, man. I don't want to see you go down."

"Appreciate it, brother. I owe you." I wasted no time rounding the brothers up and rolling out.

We rode up on the warehouse in three and a half minutes. My only objective was to take out everyone inside and get back home.

We were spread out around the house and not backing down. There was going to be blood spilled today, and while this may only be a battle and the start of a much bigger war, they were going to know that this island wasn't going to lie down and take it.

I walked right up to the door and put my boot to it. It opened easily enough, and I stormed in. I heard a door creak further down the hall and made my way toward it, ready, just ready.

The first idiot popped his head around the corner, and I didn't give him the chance to retreat. I fired, and he dropped.

I heard two other shots ring out and kept moving. I was going to drill a bullet in Vincent's head. I wasn't leaving here until I did.

When I came through a doorway and heard the screen door leading to the back of the house slam shut, I moved to it as quickly and quietly as I could.

Pushing the door open with my boot, I leaned back to look around the doorjamb and saw that two of our guys had Vincent pinned down and their guns aimed at him. I let the screen door slam shut behind me and loosened my posture. I wanted to look at ease when he saw me, not like I was in a hurry to blow his brains out and get the fuck out of there before the LEOs showed up.

I nodded to the men and said, "Let 'em up. I want him to run, so I can tell everyone how he ran from us and was too pussy to fight like a man. Beating pretty girls with pink hair and shooting old men. Can't fight a man your own size, can you, hombre?"

I watched in disgust as he rose to his feet and lifted his head to take me in.

"Right. Take a good look at me, motherfucker, because mine is the last face you're ever going to see."

Vincent's lip curled, and he said, "Kill me. More will come. My boss wants Galveston, and what he wants, he gets."

"See, man, I was willing to live and let live as long as you were staying in your own neighborhood. I didn't like it, but it was the agreement. But you took my family, and when you did that, you brought the worst of us down on you. I hope you burn in hell, you miserable piece of shit."

I lifted my gun and fired, bringing an end to a life that had no business existing in the first place.

I looked up to see that all of the men who had come along for the ride were standing around watching me, waiting for what, I wasn't sure, but I nodded my head and said, "Alright, brothers. Let's get the fuck out of here."

When we were far enough away that we wouldn't look suspicious, I pulled to the shoulder and called Alabama.

"It's done, brother. I owe you."

"We're three minutes out. Are you and your boys clear?"

"We are, and I hate that you're going to be up all night, clearing away dead criminals, but I'm really thankful to you for giving him to me. That debt? I won't ever be able to repay."

Alabama paused for a weighted moment and then said softly before disconnecting the call, "Brother, you don't owe me shit. We became family on a creek bank twenty-two years ago, and nothing will ever change that. Go home and hug your girl, tell her she's got to meet me soon, and let Nome and Scratch know. Anything, man, just let me know."

I put my phone back in my shirt pocket and grabbed a smoke. I knew that today was only the tip of the iceberg, but it felt good to have a check in the win column. To be able to go home and tell Roxanne that she wasn't confined any longer and that we could try and live a semi-normal life before things flared up around us again.

EPILOGUE

Roxanne

One by one, the men trickled in from the raid they had known was coming at any point but hadn't been able to plan in advance knowing that the guy who put a price on mine and Zeus' heads was deep in hiding.

Every time the door opened, I jerked up and waited to see if my particular tatted biker was going to be the one walking through the door. So far, he hadn't, and the longer I waited, the more scared I got.

At this point, my nerves had become contagious because Zeus was pacing looking for Jinx. I was trying to breathe while waiting. People were milling around, and no one seemed to be going anywhere anytime soon. I knew logically that they wouldn't have just shown up without saying anything if something had happened to their president, but panic and logic rarely go hand in hand.

When the door opened again, and he was the one to cross the threshold, I found that I couldn't move. Zeus didn't have the same issues, though. He caught Jinx's scent or caught sight of him and woofed in greeting. That was when Zeus finally calmed and did his three turns and plopped down with a sigh.

I gave him time. Now that I knew he was safe, I could

relax back against the couch and give him time.

Birdie came over and sat next to me. She didn't say anything for a moment, and then she patted my leg in affection and declared, "You know, you're great for him, and you're great for us. You, youngsters, are making this club really about family again, and even with all the bad right now, maybe especially, it's a wonderful thing."

My heart warmed, and I reached a hand out, laid it over hers, and squeezed in affection.

Things weren't perfect. Not anywhere close to it.

Pops and Maisie were both still in the hospital and wouldn't be getting out for at least a few days, and Maisie had a long road ahead of her.

Mitchey and Nomad were tighter than ever, but she was terrified and still jumped when one of the boys raised his voice or moved in her direction too quickly.

Things were going to heat up again with the cartel. My bikers knew that something like this wouldn't be the end but rather a shot across the bow.

But, looking up and finding Jinx smiling in my direction, I knew without a doubt that every single moment would be worth it in the end. We would get to the other side and look back on this one day and see that this was our beginning. The club would heal, we would protect each other harder than ever, and we would see it through to the other side as a family.

MISCHIEF MAKERS MOTORCYCLE CLUB

MISCHIEF MAKERS MC CONTINUES WITH NOMAD AND MITCHEY'S STORY

NOMAD

A cartel princess on the run

Micheline Maldonado is terrified and fleeing for her life. She knows what's at stake if she gets caught and she'd rather die. Her past is catching up, the danger breathing down her neck, and she's running out of options fast. Getting picked up by the handsome truck driver may be just what she needs, as long as she can avoid falling for his charming ways.

A trucker always on the move

Nomad is the black sheep of the Mischief Makers Motorcycle Club, the younger brother of the Prez, and the one his MC brothers love to hate. Most days he's good with that, but with his family in danger and the lives of people he cares for on the line, his nomadic lifestyle is stopped in its tracks. The last thing he has time for is a beautiful hitchhiker running for her life. At least, that's what he's telling himself.

An enemy bent on destruction

Even as the unlikely pair give in to their emotions, the enemy is preparing to strike from all sides.

And this time, lives will be lost.

ABOUT THE AUTHOR

Flora Burgos is a romance author from the great state of Texas. She found reading at a very tender age, devouring the bodice rippers of yore, long before she ever even had her first kiss. After an unconventional childhood and tons of travel, she is now a 30-something that steps to her own beat, just that little bit past normal. She's a modern-day hippie, with the heart of a gypsy and the soul of a dreamer and a love for animals and words that mere words do not do justice to. She has an eclectic playlist containing everything from film scores to hip hop and country to hair bands with any and everything in between. She curses like a sailor, is addicted to coffee and diet coke, loves her pit bull, hubby, and preteen son more than anything else in the world and spends her limited free time, when not reading or writing, in the kitchen with her guys where they enjoy cook-ing as a family.

Manufactured by Amazon.ca
Bolton, ON

34372753R00088